Catherine Odlum

The Life and Adventures of Prof. Robert Emmet Odlum

Containing an Account of His Splendid Natatorium at the National Capital..

Catherine Odlum

The Life and Adventures of Prof. Robert Emmet Odlum
Containing an Account of His Splendid Natatorium at the National Capital..

ISBN/EAN: 9783337179076

Printed in Europe, USA, Canada, Australia, Japan

Cover: Foto ©Raphael Reischuk / pixelio.de

More available books at **www.hansebooks.com**

THE

LIFE AND ADVENTURES

OF

Prof. Robert Emmet Odlum

CONTAINING AN ACCOUNT OF HIS

SPLENDID NATATORIUM AT THE NATIONAL CAPITAL.

His Diary—The Swimming Drill, illustrated—Reminiscences
of Great Swimmers—Stories of the Land and Sea—His
Great Swims, Jumps, &c., with the Letters of
Thanks from Persons he Rescued from
Watery Graves—The Life-Sav-
ing Service, &c., &c.

Together With Other Valuable Information.

BY HIS MOTHER,

MRS. CATHERINE ODLUM.

———

WASHINGTON, D. C.
GRAY & CLARKSON, PRINTERS.
1885.

TO THE FRIENDS OF MY LAMENTED SON,

WHOSE DEVOTION TO HIS MEMORY AFTER DEATH

PROVED THEIR TRUE FRIENDSHIP,

THIS VOLUME IS GRATEFULLY DEDICATED BY

THE AUTHOR.

PREFACE.

Though many notices have appeared in the public press of the country of the late Robert Emmet Odlum, nothing approaching to a life of the deceased has been published. That task has been assigned me. I am his disconsolate mother, and having access to all his papers and memoranda, preserved by him with great care, I am enabled to place an authentic biography before the reader.

A pride for his profession and a desire for pecuniary gain, which would better his fortunes and free him from the embarrassments of financial trouble, may have impelled him to make the fearful leap; but it was no foolhardy act, for a nobler motive also actuated him, and he has left the world the wiser for his daring deed.

The bravery he displayed will be a matter of history, and in after years, when the story of the great bridge connecting the two mighty cities is told, the tale will be incomplete without recounting the sad legend of Odlum's leap.

CATHERINE ODLUM.

INTRODUCTION.

At this time, when the sorrow-stricken relatives and mourning friends stand by the newly-made grave of Robert Emmet Odlum, the world asks: "What motive had he for the act of jumping from the Brooklyn bridge?"

A man is supposed to have a motive for everything he does. Certainly Professor Odlum had one, and he made it known to his friends more than two years ago.

It has been accepted by many, even those learned in the sciences, that death would result from passing through the air in falling or jumping from any considerable height—that life would be extinct before reaching the surface of the earth. This Professor Odlum denied. He contended there was no danger in the air in jumping from any ordinary height into the water, but that the injury, if any, resulted from a contact with the water, in failing to strike it feet foremost.

"In cases of fire," said the Professor, "persons might jump from the roofs of any building in any city, or even be thrown from the windows, into a net-work (which all public resorts and tenement-houses should keep on hand) with comparative safety. It would cost but little," said the Professor, "and thousands of lives might be saved every year. But for the fear of being killed in the air they are afraid to jump."

Apart from the fact of his pride as an athlete, and of his longing to perform a feat of daring which would have rendered him famous if it had been successful, it was to demonstrate the truth of his theory that Professor Odlum leaped from the great bridge in the presence of thousands. His physical condition or nervousness, engendered by his excitement of evading the bridge police, or currents of air, caused him to lose his balance when within about thirty feet of the water, and he fell upon his side. His passage through the air did not rob him of his breath—did not kill him—for after the jump he manifested some curiosity and asked whether he had made a good one. He tried to steady his head and to wipe the far-away look from his eyes. Only the writer knows the meaning of that look—far away from home and mother, among strangers to die. He had established the great fact, even with the sacrifice of his bright and sunny life.

His body will sleep in the City of Silence, where faithful friends and loving hearts have consigned it, but the grand fact is left as a legacy to mankind. The thousands of lives which may be saved from burning buildings by the jump and the network will show that Professor Odlum did not die in vain.

LIFE AND ADVENTURES

OF

PROF. ROBERT EMMET ODLUM.

CHAPTER I.

It is an old adage that "Death loves a shining mark." In Washington the people are often called upon to mourn the death of some great public character—some statesman whose oratory has commanded Senates, or some old warrior who once led armed hosts to battle and to victory. The flag is placed at half-mast; the Departments are clothed in mourning—their doors closed and business suspended—but not a tear is shed and a cold formality marks the proceedings. How different was the feeling on Tuesday night, the 19th of May, 1885, when the sad words were flashed over the wires from New York: "Bob Odlum jumped from the Brooklyn bridge this evening and is dead." A genuine, heartfelt sorrow filled the breasts of thousands, for Professor Odlum could number his friends by thousands, and the desire to learn the particulars caused a greater demand for the coming morrow's news. Early dawn brought a confirmation of the sad intelligence, and a feeling of admiration for the bravery of the hero lessened the grief for his death. Men spoke in glowing terms of the daring of the man who could undertake the hazardous leap with a smile on his brow. To let himself be fully understood, the Professor is said to have told a *Herald* reporter a few hours before his jump: "If I should die, I don't want the public to think I had no good object in view. I want the *Herald* to explain that I have for years illustrated the fact that men do not die while falling through the air; and no matter if men or women were one hundred feet high on the roof of a burning building they would not hesitate to jump into a net if they read that I had jumped one hundred and forty feet from the Brooklyn bridge."

Robert Emmet Odlum was born in Ogdensburgh, N. Y., August 31, 1851, and was consequently in his thirty-fourth year. From his very earliest infancy he exhibited an aptitude for the water, and even in his childhood acquired the fame of a bold and expert swimmer. In his boyhood it was his delight to buffet the waves and tides of the Mississippi for many hours each day, and to swim and dive the happy hours away. He almost lived in the water, and I have heard many incidents related of his feats. Among them I recall his chase of a wounded wild duck that had been shot through the wing and could not fly, but dived and swam for seven miles on the Mississippi. The duck would dive and young Odlum would follow suit, until at last he captured and bore the duck home in triumph. The water seemed to be his natural element.

Many years of the life of young Odlum were spent in the South, where he is fondly remembered and sincerely mourned by a host of friends. There are many brave acts of his known to friends in the South that have never appeared in public print. Wherever he lived he made friends, and no word was ever said to his discredit.

CHAPTER II.

About seven years ago Prof. Odlum came to this
city from Chicago, where he had been employed on
the press of that city, and made for himself quite
a reputation for energy and ability. He proposed
the establishment of a great Natatorium, and was
warmly seconded and indorsed by the journals and
public-spirited citizens of Washington. In a short
space of time he had perfected the largest and
most complete swimming school in this country,
and fitted it up at a cost of over $20,000. Every
convenience in the way of bathing suits, dressing
rooms, &c., were furnished the pupils.

One of the most graceful and expert swimmers
who attended the Natatorium at the commencement
was Miss Sallie Horner, daughter of Judge Horner. Miss Horner was a perfect adept in the art,
and executed diving and all of the fancy feats of the
natatorial science with the utmost ease and facility.
Miss Fannie Hayes, daughter of ex-President
Hayes, was among the distinguished pupils. Prof.
Odlum was perfect master of his profession, and
his exhibitions of the natatorial art were intensely
interesting. He would dive in the basin of the
Natatorium, and while under the water completely
change his bathing suit and appear after a few
minutes arrayed in an entirely different suit.
Washington was completely carried away with the
swimming school, and scholars flocked around the
Professor. One enthusiastic newspaper reporter
declared "that the Professor would live in the
memory and esteem of future ages on account of
the magnanimous spirit which prompted him to
erect in the heart of our city a cooling fountain

wherein the weary and worn may, during the
heated term, recuperate the exhausted powers of
nature by a refreshing bath.''

The sons of Presidents Hayes and Garfield were
his pupils, as also the sons of Hon. J. G. Blaine,
General Sherman, and the *elite* of the metropolis.
The reporters of the press vied with each other as
to who could say the most complimentary things
about the Professor and his Natatorium.

The correspondent of a prominent journal of
Burlington, (*Hawkeye,*) Iowa, writes:

''Ladies bathe in the cooling waters of the
Natatorium where thousands learn to swim. The
school is patronized by the best people of the city.
Mrs. Truckson, the daughter of General Sherman,
is one of the pupils of Professor Odlum. She is tall,
with pale, golden hair, and blue eyes. She was lately
married, and is amiable and sweet tempered. It
is funny to see Professor Odlum take a new pupil
into the water, with her pretty little shrieks,
as she looks down into the artificial lake about
three feet deep. A strap is belted around the
chest, attached to a pole, with a hook inserted into
this belt, and, when the Professor pulls her along
in the water, she looks like a frog, but with red legs,
as most of the ladies wear red stockings. Those
who are experts dive off a spring-board into a
deeper basin, with a chug and a dash, disappear,
and rise like Venus in the foam of the sea, drip-
ping, their bathing suits clinging to them like—
well, a wet blanket. Bathing suits are mostly
made of gray flannel trimmed with red *galloon*,
and in half bloomer style. No gentlemen are admitted excepting Professor Odlum, or a man and
his wife.''

Descriptions of the Natatorium were published
in all the city papers. Everything there was ar-

ranged in the most orderly and cleanly manner. It was truly the greatest swimming school in the world. A great volume of fresh water was constantly pouring into the basin, and this changed and purified it. Every precaution for safety was used, and those who patronized the school were taught by Professor Odlum to become such expert swimmers that they apparently lived in the water with as much ease as out of it. In this model school swimming was not only taught as a useful art but as a graceful accomplishment, and only those who have seen an expert know its possibilities in this respect. No doubt it is on this account that the accomplishment became so fashionable and is so much affected by young ladies in society.

CHAPTER III.

During the winter months of '80 and '81 Professor Odlum added many conveniences to his splendid Natatorium, and in April, 1881,

THE SWIMMING SEASON OPENED

with great eclat. We give the following account from the Washington *Post* of April, 1881, which will be read with interest:

Interesting Opening Exercises at the Natatorium.

An event in the social life of the capital city was the opening of the season at the Washington Natatorium, so ably managed for the past three years by Prof. R. E. Odlum, one of the best swimmers in the country, and a most successful instructor, yesterday morning. The large and neat establishment was thronged with ladies from the foremost circles of society, prominent in the assemblage being the wife of President Garfield and the families of several Cabinet officers and prominent Senators. The visitors were finely entertained by the Professor and a score of his expert scholars—ladies and gentlemen. The best of the lady swimmers was the wife of a well-known newspaper correspondent. At night the place was again crowded, and the many gentlemen present enjoyed the wonderful feats of the Professor and several of his male scholars. At both entertainments the majority of the spectators were graduates of the institution, and their kindly recognition of their teacher, Professor Odlum, spoke volumes in his favor. In conversation with the Professor, he stated that under his instruction fully 700 ladies and five times as many gentlemen in Washington had become expert swimmers. He pronounces it easier to teach a woman than a man, but the women never become as proficient in the art. Women are the best floaters, however—you can hardly keep them under water. Washington city has more good lady swimmers than any city in the country, New York not excepted. One of the Professor's best scholars was the daughter of Mr. Hayes, who became a very fine swimmer. The interest manifested this year, he says, is far greater than at the commencement of any previous season. Professor Odlum has swam twelve miles without a rest, and has remained under the water for three minutes and ten seconds. For the last feat he was presented with a magnificent gold medal. He has dived from a point eighty feet above the surface of the water, and he intends, some time this summer, to dive from the highest point of the great St. Louis bridge—over 110 feet above the surface of the Mississippi river. This will be the greatest dive on record. The Professor is certain to receive most liberal patronage this season, and he deserves success.

The season was propitious, and the liberal inducements offered and the utmost confidence reposed in the Professor secured for him a full school of enthusiastic pupils. His proposition to teach the art of swimming to the most timid persons in eight or ten lessons was a popular one, and in every instance he fulfilled his promise.

To the swimming school he now attached a gymnasium, which was a favorite resort, but whether it added to his financial success is doubted. His fame has gone forth throughout the land, and he was universally admitted to be the champion swimmer and diver of the world. His ambition yearned for something greater than the proprietorship of the National Natatorium. He desired some broader, deeper stream than the Natatorium. He wished to buffet the waves of Old Ocean, and ride like Neptune upon the angry billows and laugh at the sound of the sea.

CHAPTER IV.

About the 7th of May, 1881, notwithstanding the success of his Natatorium, we find Professor Odlum growing restless in his position as proprietor of his school. His ambition sought a more extended field of operation. He was conscious of his

2

skill; his friends fed the flames of his ambition, and we find that he sent a challenge for publication in the New York *Clipper*, offering to compete for from $100 to $500 in a half hour's exhibition in the water.

On the 13th of July, 1881, he challenged any man in the United States to swim him for from $250 to $500 a side. No one would accept the wager offered. It was a bet, as the sportsmen say, "without takers," and the champion floated upon the wave without a competitor to contest the honors.

It was now the season of the year when the steamers left our wharves freighted with happy excursionists down the beautiful Potomac. There was music and .dancing, fair maidens and brave men, but the chief attraction on these occasions was the presence of "Bob" Odlum, as he was familiarly called, and his daring jumps and feats in the water. His exhibitions possessed a fascination it was impossible to resist. Once, at Marshall Hall, in 1881, he remained under the water three minutes and ten seconds, a longer time than that achieved by any swimmer in the world.

On Wednesday before the great boat race between Hanlan and Courtney, Professor Odlum swam over the entire course marked off for the oarsmen. In conversing with Hanlan and Courtney he discovered that "neither knew how to swim," which astonished him very much.

The next remarkable feat performed by Professor Odlum was on July 4, 1881, at Occoquan Falls. He happened to be one of the party aboard, and was badgered by some of his gentlemen friends about jumping from the top of the wooden bridge, . a distance of 90 feet. The Professor determined not to be bluffed, agreed to make the jump, and accomplished the feat without the slightest trepidation and in the most graceful manner.

In June, 1882, a grand excursion was announced to take place from this city to Marshall Hall. The fact that Professor Odlum and Captain Paul Boyton would give exhibitions of their skill—the former by jumping a distance of 100 feet—attracted a large crowd. On the arrival of the boat at the wharf at Marshall Hall the excitement was intense. Professor Odlum then performed a most hazardous feat. A ladder was raised upon the deck of the steamer to the height of 90 feet—making the distance to the water 110 feet—up which the Professor climbed. The strong wind caused the ladder to sway, but, nothing daunted, the Professor took the leap. He could not keep his balance, and as he cleft the air, rapidly moving his legs to prevent his falling flat upon the water, a cry of fear broke from the multitude upon the deck. When he neared the water, Odlum quickly crossed his hands over his stomach and entered the water at a slight angle. He immediately came to the surface, and after giving his wonderful exploits in the water, boarded the boat uninjured.

CHAPTER V.

Robert Emmet Odlum was too generous in his nature to retain wealth, even after acquiring it; and it was perhaps due more to this than to any other cause that the swimming school was a financial failure. There was a disagreement among the property-holders on which the Natatorium was built, the premises were offered for sale and the swimming school closed. It was then that the announcement was made that Professor Odlum had been employed at Fortress Monroe, where we propose to follow him. It was there that he made the great swim from the beach to Ocean View, nine miles and back, in a rough sea. It was there he saved the lives of several persons from watery graves. It was there he made for himself a reputation as a great swimmer and diver. It was there he received testimonials from grateful hearts for services performed, which he treasured above all he possessed. Some of these letters we print to show the disposition of the deceased. He saved human life—deemed it but his duty and said nothing about it. In one instance he hardly received thanks. Comment is unnecessary. The coming chapter will reveal the story. The world can read and draw its own conclusions. It is not the first instance on record where ingratitude was the only reward for a favor received.

The Fortress Monroe correspondent of the *National Republican*, under date of August 16, 1882, writes:

"On Thursday, August 10, R. E. Odlum, of Washington, D. C., professor of swimming at the Hygeia Hotel, Fortress Monroe, accomplished the very difficult feat of swimming to Ocean View and back, a distance of eighteen miles. He started at 12 o'clock and was watched by the bathers until his red cap faded in the distance, and arrived at Ocean View at 2:40 p. m., making the nine miles in two hours and forty minutes. After resting an hour and a half the Professor entered the water, gave an exhibition of fancy swimming, diving, floating, etc., and at 5 p. m., amid hearty cheers from the crowd on the beach, he started for Fort-

ress Monroe. He arrived at the Hygeia Hotel at
8:25 p. m., making the longest swim ever made in
this country ; and when it is considered that for the
last half hour .he was compelled to swim dead
against the tide in Hampton Roads, too much cannot be said of his ability as a swimmer."

This is only the comment of one correspondent.
The Washington *Post*, of August 13, 1882, in
commenting on the great swim, says :

" Professor R. E. Odlum, well known in this
city, accomplished a splendid swimming feat last
Thursday. A wager of $100 was made that he
could not swim, without the aid of a boat,
from Old Point Comfort to Ocean View, a distance
variously estimated at nine miles, inside of three
hours. He started from the Hygeia Hotel at 12
o'clock noon and arrived at Ocean View at 2:40.
He rested at that place for one hour and a half,
and then entered the water, giving the residents at
Ocean View an exhibition swim. At 5:30 p. m.
he commenced his return trip, without a boat, to
Fortress Monroe, where he landed at 8:25 p. m. in
good condition. The feat created considerable enthusiasm at Old Point, and the professor was the
recipient of numerous congratulations."

The Sunday *Gazette, Chronicle, Capital* and other
city papers noticed the remarkable swim in terms
complimentary to Professor Odlum, and the Norfolk *Landmark,* in speaking of the event, says :
" The only difficulty the Professor experienced
during his long and splendid swim was in striking
a school of sea-nettles, which made it warm for a
time."

The Fortress Monroe correspondent of the Norfolk *Landmark* of July 6, 1882, writes as follows :
" The people here grow eloquent over the heroic
work performed by Bob Odlum in saving three

lives at this place. The first person rescued was 'Sky' Colfax, the sixteen-year-old son of ex-Vice-President Colfax. He jumped from the wharf and was carried away by the strong current. After battling for life, he at last called for assistance, when Bob plunged in and rescued him, just as he sank. Had it not been for this timely assistance 'Sky' would have ascended to the skies. Bob also rescued Mr. T. Cooley, of Nashville, Tenn., and Mr. Morton, of Kentucky."

The Norfolk *Landmark* correspondent of July 22, 1882, in his letter from Fortress Monroe, says:

"At the Hygeia Hotel, where hundreds of amphibiously-inclined guests go in bathing every day, no accident has ever happened to mar the season's pleasure. It is not because the visitors are more experienced or less reckless in the water, but owing to the fact that a competent person is here in the dual capacity of manager of the swimming-school and life-guard on the beach. Mr. R. E. Odlum, who is the gentleman in question, contributes a great deal by his presence to one of the most delightful enjoyments with which a holiday at the seaside is associated, for one feels so much more at ease when he knows that a willing arm is ready to come to his assistance. Mr. Odlum, or Bob, as he is familiarly called, has saved

THE LIVES OF THREE PERSONS

this summer. The first was that of 'Sky' Colfax, a bright, handsome, sixteen-year-old son of Hon. Schuyler Colfax. This young American had too much confidence in his swimming abilities, and was bold enough to jump from the wharf, not taking into consideration how strong the tide was running. After making a long effort to reach shore, fighting

against the rapid current, and too proud to call for
assistance, the boy found himself in an exhausted
condition, and feebly called for help.   His father,
who was standing on the wharf, did not know until his son gave the alarm that he was in distress.
The Hon. Schuyler could not swim and thought
his son was doing nicely until the cry for aid
reached his ear.   Then, with a terrified look, he
turned to seek assistance, when the welcome sight
of Odlum running down the wharf and pulling off
his coat the while met his eye.   Mr. Odlum, fortunately, had seen the boy's danger from the hotel
and immediately rushed to the rescue.   Taking a
header, he quickly sped to the drowning boy's assistance, who sank just before Bob reached him, but
he was quickly brought to the surface, and shortly
after put in the loving arms of his father, a crest-
fallen but it is hoped a more discreet boy.

"The second instance was that of Mr. T. Cooley,
of Nashville, Tenn., who is a fair swimmer, but
sometimes suffers from an attack of sunstroke he
received last summer, and it was while swimming
some distance from shore that the last attack came
on him.

"THE CRY OF ALARM WAS SOUNDED,

and again Odlum came to the front, reaching Mr.
Cooley in time to bring him safely to the beach and
receive the congratulations of the hundreds of persons who saw the act.

"The last brave performance of this young man
was that of yesterday, when he saved Mr. A. M.
Morton, of Shelby county, Ky., from drowning.
This gentleman had ventured out too far, and not
being able to swim, the strong tide took him off his
feet.   His struggles to regain a footing were un-

successful, and slowly but surely he was drifting under water and away. Once more the powerful stroke of Mr. Odlum's arm sped him on his life-saving mission, and once more he was successful."

Since the death of Captain Webb, Professor Odlum was known and recognized as the champion swimmer of the world. The Washington *Evening Star* of the 15th of August, 1882, says:

"It will be remembered that R. E. Odlum, of Washington, swam nine miles at Fortress Monroe in two hours and thirty minutes on Thursday, beating Captain Webb's time by two and a half minutes."

CHAPTER VI.

THE ART OF SWIMMING.

To show the aquatic propensity of Professor Odlum one need only read his "diary," in which he penned his thoughts and cut and pasted every item concerning the exploits of swimmers and divers, and even the habits of sharks and other monsters of the deep. He loved to read of the Patagonians who threw their children into the sea, and then rescuing them when they could not help themselves. A familiarity with the water he contended was necessary to mankind—the art of swimming should be a part of the education of every child of both sexes. If his advice should be adopted by mankind generally, very few would find watery graves, and the wild winds and mad waves, shipwrecks and storms would lose half

their terrors; fewer forms would rest upon the
beds of green sea-flowers that blossom down
fathoms below the surface of the ocean; and the
red coral would no longer grow around the skulls
of the dead; the boy would no longer stand upon
the burning deck, but with the knowledge of the
art of swimming would plunge in the sea—fearless
and free from alarm.

"Learn to swim," said Professor Odlum, "for
neither Providence nor fate is always to be tempted
by dereliction of duty or neglect of precaution.
The numerous late disasters on our favorite boats
for summer travel and excursions would have
been devoid of its fearful loss of life did people
only possess the slightest knowledge of 'knowing how to swim.'

"Within easy reach of succor, with friendly boats
and steamers coming to assistance, many unfortunates, nevertheless, perished—a sad commentary—
not even being able to make an effort to keep afloat
for a few seconds; to sink without a struggle to pro-
pel the body by the limbs with which the Creator
endowed him. Coroners' juries may make their pro-
test—of what avail is it to the dead? Steamboat
captains and companies may be punished for culpa-
ble carelessness—can it restore life? Is it not wiser
to guard against accidents of this nature by a
few practical lessons in the art of swimming?
Remember that only a slight knowledge of it imparts confidence and coolness—an essential quality
in moments of danger.

"I do not say this as an advertisement for my
own gain, but to benefit others. The New York
papers since the frightful steamboat disasters, in
none of which need any one have been lost if proficient in the art of swimming, are printing the
maxim: 'Every boy should learn to swim.' Every

girl should learn to swim also." Any person may become proficient by learning the following

PRACTICAL LESSONS ON SWIMMING.

Swimming has now become an art, and certain rules may be given for its attainment, by the aid of which, and a little practice, the most timid may eventually acquire the delightful power of " sporting in the silver flood." In addition to its advantages as a healthy and bracing exercise, humanity is one ; the pleasure of being not only able to preserve our own lives, but those of others, ought certainly to be sufficient inducement to acquire a dexterity in this most useful art.

The only obstacle to improvement in this necessary and life-preserving art is fear, and it is only by overcoming this timidity that you can expect to become a master. But you will be no swimmer till you can place confidence in the power of the water to support you.

ENTERING THE WATER.

A young pupil must not at first venture into the water in the bold and dashing manner of experienced swimmers. He must wait patiently until he can do so without danger. Let him remember that there has been a time when the best swimmer alive tottered, step by step, into the water, and sounded the depth with one foot before he lifted the other from the bottom of the stream. Leander himself, with whose history and fate our juvenile readers who are tolerably advanced in the classics are doubtless acquainted—Leander himself, we repeat, who so often swam across the Hellespont, once paddled in a pond, and those who, under their directions, make their first attempt to buoy themselves up by their own natural powers in a shallow brook, may hereafter become lusty swimmers enough to perform the same feat of which Lord Byron was so proud. Our young friend should be patient as well as persevering during his probation in the art of swimming. He must not feel disgusted and disheartened because he seems to make comparatively but little progress. Let him remember that he is gradually acquiring a new and most important power, and is by degrees obtaining a mastery over the waters. It was well observed by a writer of great discernment that nothing which is worth learning is compassed without some difficulty and application ; that it is well worth some pains and trouble to render one's self fearless of falling into a river, in which two out of three of our fellow-countrymen would, in a similar situation, without assistance, be drowned, must be admitted. Let not that trouble therefore be grudged.

Previously to entering the water the head and neck should be well wetted ; the pupil should then advance by a clear shelving bank in some stream, the depth of which he has ascertained by plumbing or otherwise until he is breast high ; then let him face about toward the bank and prepare to make his first essay in the art of

STRIKING OUT.

With his face turned toward the bank, as above directed, let the pupil lie down gently on his breast, keep his head and neck upright, his breast advanced, and his back bent inward. Then let him withdraw his legs from the bottom and immediately strike them out, not downward, but behind him ; strike out the arms forward, with the palms

closed and the backs uppermost a little below the
surface of the water ; draw them back again while
he is gathering up his legs for a second attempt,
and thus push forward, making use of his hands
and feet alternately. It will, perhaps, happen that
he will swallow water in his first efforts, but this
should not discourage him ; neither should he
fancy that because he makes but little advance he
is not as capable of learning to swim as well as
others—the same little mishaps occur to all young
beginners.

The writer of these pages has buffeted the billows miles from land, where the waters have been
moved by what an angler calls a curling breeze,
with a pleasure which those, and those alone, who
have reveled in the strong bosom of the sea can
imagine ; and what is more difficult, he has swam
the still, torpid deeps of an inland lake in a dead
calm. And this is the manner which he has
always followed, and which he recommends his
young friends to adopt, of striking out with the
arms: The fingers are to be closed and the thumbs
kept close to the hand, which should be straightened, or rather, a little hollowed in the palm ; the
hands are then to be brought together, the thumbs
touching, or palm to palm—it is little matter
which—and raised just under the chin ; they are
then to be struck vigorously forward, and when the
arms are at their full stretch parted, and carried,
slowly and regularly, a little below the surface of
the water, at the full stretch of the arms, backward as far as convenience will permit ; they
should then sink toward the hips ; by a slight
pressure on the water, as they descend, the body
will be raised, the head may be thrown back and
the breath drawn in for the next stroke. When
the hands are at or near the hips, they should be

raised, with the thumbs or edges, but by no means the backs, upward to the first position; while doing this, the legs are to be drawn up as near the body as possible, and the soles of the feet struck out against the water with reasonable force at the same moment the hands are thrust forward again. This is, in fact, the whole principle of swimming: the arms are first thrust forward and the body propelled by the force of the soles of the feet striking against the water; the air in the lungs is expired or breathed forth during this action; the hands are then stretched out and carried around so as to lift the body (which wants no support during the time it is propelled by the legs and the lungs are nearly full of air) while the legs are drawn up and the lungs filled with air for a second effort. These very simple motions will seem difficult and complicated to the young swimmer at first, but by degrees he will learn to perform them with facility. Above all things let him endeavor to do them deliberately and without being flurried. It is a fact that a swimmer who is apparently slow in his action makes more progress by half than one who is quick. The former is deliberate and vigorous; the latter hurried, less effectual, and soon becomes fatigued. A tyro in the art will make ten efforts during the time occupied by an adept in performing one, and at the same time will scarcely make one-half the progress.

TO TREAD WATER.

All that is necessary for treading water is to let your legs drop in the water until you are upright; then keep yourself afloat in that position by treading downward with your feet, alternately, and, if necessary, paddling with your palms at your hips.

TO SWIM ON THE SIDE.

Lower your left side and at the same time elevate your right; strike forward with your left hand and sideway with your right, the back of the latter being in front instead of upward, the thumb side of the hand downward, so as to serve precisely as an oar. You will thus, by giving your body an additional impetus, advance much more speedily than in the common way. It will also relieve you considerably when you feel tired of striking out forward. You may also turn on the right side, strike out with the right hand, and use the left as an oar. In either case the action of the legs is the same as usual.

THE PORPOISE.

This is a very pleasant and most advantageous change of action. The right arm is lifted entirely out of the water, the shoulder thrust forward, and the swimmer, while striking out with his legs, reaches forward with his hand as far as possible. At the utmost stretch of the arm the hand falls, a little hollowed, into the water, which it grasps or pulls toward the swimmer in its return to the body, in a transverse direction, toward the other armpit. While it is passing through the water in this manner, the legs are drawn up for another effort, and the left arm and shoulder elevated and thrust forward as above directed for the right. This is the greatest advancing relief in swimming, except swimming on the back. Floating on the back rests the whole of the body as well as the limbs, but while floating no progress is made ; whereas during the time a person swims in the manner above directed he will not only relieve himself considerably, but also make as great an advance in the water as if he were preceding in the ordinary way.

TO SWIM AND FLOAT ON THE BACK.

To do this you must turn yourself on your back as gently as possible, elevate your breast above the surface, put your head back, so that your eyes, nose, mouth and chin only are above water. By keeping in this position with the legs and arms extended and paddling the hands gently by the side of the hips you will float. If you wish to swim, you must strike out with the legs, taking care not to lift your knees too high nor sink your hips and sides too low, but keeping in as straight a line as possible. You may lay the arms across the breast, keep them motionless at the sides, or, if you wish, strike out with them to help you on.

To swim with your feet forward while on your back, lift up your legs one after another, let them fall into the water, and draw them back with all the force you can toward your hams, thus you will swim feet forward and return to the place whence you came.

To turn from your breast to your back, raise your legs forward and throw your head backward, until your body is in a right position ; to change from the back to the breast, drop your legs and throw your body forward on your breast.

TO TURN WHEN SWIMMING.

If you wish to turn while on your back, keep one leg still and embrace the water beside you with the other, thus you will find yourself turn to that side on which your leg by its motion embraces the water, and you will turn either to the right or left, according to which leg you use in this manner.

To turn while swimming in the ordinary way requires no further effort than to incline your head and body to the side you would turn to, and, at the same time, move and turn your legs in the same manner as you would do to turn the same way on land.

TO SHOW THE FEET.

While on your back bend the small of it downward, support yourself by moving your hands to and fro just above your breast, and stretch your feet above the water.

TO BEAT THE WATER, ETC.

When swimming on your back, lift your legs out of the water one after another, and strike the water with them alternately. Those who are most expert at this bring their chins toward their breasts at each stroke of the legs.

There is a variety of similar feats performed by expert swimmers, such as treading water with both hands raised over the head; floating on the back with the arms above the surface; taking the left leg in the right hand out of the water when swimming on the back; pulling the right heel by the right hand toward the back when swimming in the common way; throwing somersets in the water, backward and forward, &c., for which no particular directions are necessary, as the pupil when he has grown expert in the various modes of swimming which have been described will be able to do these things, and any tricks which his fancy may suggest, without difficulty.

DIVING.

Diving, by practice, may be carried to astonishing perfection. Pearls are brought up from the bottom of the sea by divers who are trained to remain a considerable time under water. In ancient times divers were employed in war to destroy the ships of the enemy, and many instances are related by respectable authors of men diving after and fetching up nails and pieces of money thrown into the sea, and even overtaking the nail or coin before it has reached the bottom.

Diving may be performed from the surface of the water, when swimming, by merely turning the head downward, and striking upward with the legs. It is, however, much better to leap in, with the hands closed above the head, and head foremost, from a pier, boat or raised bank. By merely striking with the feet, and keeping his head toward the bottom, the diver may drive himself a considerable distance beneath the surface. If he reach the bottom, he has only to turn his head upward, spring from the ground with his feet, and he will soon arrive at the surface. If desirous of making a more rapid ascent, he should strike downward with his feet, pulling the water above him toward his head with one hand, and striking it downward by his side with the other. In diving, the eyes should be open; you must, therefore, take care that you do not close them, as they reach the surface, when you commence your descent. It is almost needless to add, that the breath should be held the whole time that you are under water.

SWIMMING UNDER WATER.

Swimming between top and bottom may be ac-

3

complished by the ordinary stroke, if you take
care to keep your head a little downward, and strike
a little higher with your feet than when swimming
on the surface; or, you may turn your thumbs
downward, and perform the stroke with the hands
in that position, instead of keeping them flat.

THE CRAMP.

These practical directions in the art of swimming
would be incomplete without saying a few words as
to the cramp. Those who are at all liable to it
ought, perhaps, to abandon all idea of swimming;
men of the greatest skill as swimmers, and of presence of mind in danger, have fallen victims to this,
which has been well enough called, "the bathers'
bane." The cramp may, however, seize a person
for the first time in his life when at a distance from
land; this has frequently been known to occur,
but the sufferer can save himself if he should ever
be seized with this terrible contraction. Be assured
that there is no danger, if you are only a tolerable
swimmer and do not flurry yourself. The moment
you feel the cramp in your leg or foot, strike out
the limb with all your strength, thrusting the heel
out, and drawing the toes upward as forcibly as possible, totally regardless of the momentary pain it
may occasion. If two or three efforts of this nature
do not succeed, throw yourself on your back, and
endeavor to keep yourself afloat with your hands
until assistance reach you; or, if there be no hope
of that, try to paddle ashore with your palms.
Should you be unable to float on your back, put
yourself in the position directed for treading water,
and you may keep your head above the surface by
merely striking the water downward with your
hands at your hips, without any assistance from

your legs. In case you have the cramp in both legs, you may also endeavor to make some progress in this manner, should no help be at hand. If you have one leg only attacked, you may drive yourself forward with the other. In order to endow you with confidence in a moment of danger from an attack of the cramp, occasionally try to swim with one leg, or a leg and a hand, or the two hands only, and you will find that it is by no means difficult.

CONCLUDING REMARKS.

In entering the water, the head should be wetted first, either by plunging in head foremost, or pouring water on it. Before you adopt the first method, ascertain if the water be sufficiently deep to allow you to dive without touching the bottom, otherwise you may injure yourself against it. Do not remain in the water too long, but come out as soon as you feel tired, chilly or numbed. It is a good plan to make a plunge, so as to wet the body all over, to return to shore immediately, and an instant afterward enter the water at your ease, and take your lesson or your swim. You do not feel so chilly if you do this, as if you dash in and swim off at once. Never be alarmed at having a few mouthfuls of water when learning to swim ; be not discouraged at difficulties, but bear in mind, that millons have done what you are attempting to do. Beware of banks which have holes in them, and venture out of your depth only by degrees.

If one of your companions be in danger of drowning, be sure that, in endeavoring to save him, you make your approaches in such a manner as will prevent him from grappling with you ; if he once gets hold of your limbs, you both will almost inevitably be lost.

CHAPTER VII.

The Bible tells us that a guardian angel is appointed for each one of us. Dealings with mankind show that each mortal has an evil genius. Every one has an Eden of his own, and the devil tries to enter there. Paul Boyton was the evil genius of Professor Odlum. When he first entered Washington he found the Professor with a prosperous Natatorium, patronized by the best people of the city. The world looked fair and pleasant, no debt encumbered his affairs, and but for the entrance of this advertising humbug, how different would have been the life of Professor Odlum! Boyton came with all his plausibility as an agent of St. Jacob's Oil, and claimed the proprietorship of the stuffed whale. Like Mulberry Sellers, he boasted that "millions were in it." With his boasts of coming wealth, an easy life, and promising fame and gold in the future, he easily induced Professor Odlum to leave the "even tenor of his way." To follow the unprincipled adventurer was now his ambition, and to recover his lost means he made desperate resolves—to achieve notoriety by big jumps, such as most men would have shrank from in horror. Boyton's great schemes soon came to an end—there was no merit in them. The "stuffed whale" was pounced upon for debt, and St.. Jacob with his magic oil receded from Boyton's grasp. He was jealous of Professor Odlum and sought to make use of his attainments to enrich himself. He found ready allies in the sports of New York, who are ever on the alert for some chance to fill their depleted pockets, and enable them to live fancy and dissolute lives at the expense of the industry of others. They were familiar with the prowess possessed by Professor Odlum, had witnessed his high leaps from bridges and masts of vessels in mid ocean, had heard of his long swims and feats in the water, and here was a golden opportunity for them. The Professor was ambitious, enthusiastic withal ; and by their blandishments, encouragement and flattery induced him to conceive that wealth and fame would attend him in a grand leap from the Brooklyn bridge. So long did he ponder, that the idea grew upon him, and fastened upon his imagination like a clamp of steel ; it became the dream of his life, and the "sports," headed by Boyton, chuckled with delight as they anticipated the harvest of gold that would flow into their pockets on the success or failure of the daring of a brave young man, who unwisely termed these bloodthirsty sports his friends.

> "What is friendship? But a name—
> A charm that lulls to sleep."

But, alas! in this instance it was a sleep eternal for one he called his friend, but really his worst enemy in disguise. The jump was a desperate undertaking. In gazing down from the bridge into the East River, the passer-by is struck with wonder that there ever should have lived a man with nerve enough to plunge from its dizzy height into the river. Boyton and his sports cared nothing for the danger. Whatever injury resulted would not injure them. In the event of disaster and death, could they not easily capture the letters they had written the unfortunate man? After the catastrophe the letters disappeared, no evidence remained, and the coroner's jury would bring in a verdict, "there was no one to blame." But fortunately other testimony convicting Boyton and the sports

remained. The Professor had corresponded with
Boyton for years, as his letters will show. The letters and telegrams inviting the Professor to come
on to New York and make the jump were in possession of the Professor when he left Washington,
but got into Boyton's hands after the tragedy, and
are hidden away or destroyed. We publish in the
chapter of letters the complicity of Boyton in the sad
affair, and to convict him of a deliberate falsehood
when he penned his letter to the press declaring he
"had never written R. E. Odlum ten lines in his
life."

CHAPTER VIII.

THE DIARY OF PROFESSOR ODLUM.

The most interesting chapter of this book is the
diary left by the unfortunate Professor. In this we
find his thoughts recorded, his adventures, the
names of his friends, and articles on swimming,
diving, jumping, athletic sports, his private corre-
spondence, and reminiscences of men who have
become celebrated for the ability they have displayed in their specialties.

The following account of some of his swimming
adventures is taken from the diary. It shows a
fund of humor, and is couched in language altogether his own. The narrative is entitled—

LOOKING FOR WIGGINS' STORM.

March 11, 1883.—I left Washington last evening
on the steamer Excelsior, and this morning about

6 o'clock jumped into the Chesapeake Bay with my
rubber suit ten miles from Fortress Monroe. A
few moments after I struck the water I became
aware of the fact that my suit was leaking, because
of a cold streak across the small of my back. The
gentleman who assisted me in adjusting the suit
did not understand how to fit it in the back, and
as I was unable to inspect that part of it, was
ignorant of its condition until the leak apprised me
of the fact. I had with me in a rubber bag two
bottles of fresh water and a flask of stimulants.
When the leak filled my suit and I became thoroughly chilled, I resorted to the stimulants, but
found in a few moments that the liquor got cold in
me and made me feel worse than before I took it. So
I discontinued its use and tried to keep up circulation by vigorous paddling. The wind was very
high and against me, and the tide, which made a
chop sea, was continually breaking over my head.
After a hard pull I landed at the Hygeia Hotel,
five minutes after eleven a. m., in an exhausted
condition—wet through for five hours.

March 14.—I went into the water to-day and
gave the Hygeia guests an exhibition in my suit.
Having had three days' rest after my Sunday trip
I was feeling pretty good, and did nicely before a
large audience.

March 15.—Went into water to-day. Dumb
assistant. Suit leaked.

March 23.—Left Hygeia Hotel this morning on
the Excelsior, and am now on my way to Norfolk,
Va. I had a very pleasant time at Old Point, and
made some agreeable acquaintances; among them
Mr. Joseph Wild, importer of carpets and linoleum,

11 and 13 Thomas street, New York, who kindly
invited me to call on him.

Easter Monday, March 26.—I was advertised to
give an exhibition at Boston wharf to-day, but
owing to a wet, disagreeable day, the Norfolk people
did not turn out to a numerous extent, and after a
short swim I came out of the water soaking wet.
Another dumb assistant.

March 27.—I gave an exhibition at "Campbell's
wharf," Norfolk, to-day, after which I paddled
over to Portsmouth, where I landed to the delight
of a great crowd, answered a number of the regular questions, and then put back to my starting
place.

Friday, March 30.—At three o'clock in the afternoon I left Norfolk from Campbell's wharf on an
ebb tide for Fortress Monroe, a distance of eighteen
miles. The wind was against me, and a heavy
chop was rolling, which made it difficult to make
any progress, and it was only by hard work
that I succeeded in getting along about one mile
and a half an hour. As I passed the schooners and
ships in the Elizabeth river, which were there for
harbor and other purposes, the crews would come
to their sides and give me a cheer. About seven
o'clock I met the steam tug Germania, commanded
by a friend of mine, Capt. Sam Contain, and as a
gale was then blowing he wanted me to go back to
Norfolk with him, but I concluded to continue my
voyage in the storm. So he whistled me a salute
and we separated.

An hour later the gale had become a regular
northeaster, and the rain fell in torrents. I was
forced ashore near Craney Island, and made

application for shelter on a farm that was managed by a man named Dukes. While I was talking to some colored men who worked on the farm, explaining to them my condition, and who and what I was, Dukes called them away, but before I was left alone one of the colored men told me that there was another house a half a mile up the beach, where I could get shelter. A large dog, a savage-looking brute, then came at me, and but for the good-hearted colored man would have done me injury. I then started up the beach.

The wind was howling and the rain blowing as the big waves washed on the beach, and altogether it was a very dismal hour. But there is truth in the saying "that it is darkest before the break of day," as it was not long before I came in sight of a light shining through a window, up to which I walked, after blowing my fog horn three or four times to apprise the inmates that some one was outside, and that my appearance would not alarm them when I was seen.

In a moment the door was opened and a young man cautiously eyed me from head to foot as I informed him where I came from and that I wanted shelter. Another gentleman then stepped to the door, looked at me a few moments, and said: "Come in," and into a cheerful, large dining-room I was ushered, with a bright fire burning and the table set for supper. My good-hearted German host, Henry Kirn by name, then invited me into the kitchen to remove my rubber suit, when it was discovered that the clothes under were damp, and I was kindly furnished with dry ones; then taken into the dining-room and introduced to the family, which consisted of Mr. and Mrs. Kirn and five children—three boys and two girls. After supper I spent a very pleasant evening in general conversation, and was finally shown to the room that I was to occupy for the night. I have traveled a great deal, but I never before nor never again expect to find myself the occupant of such a luxuriant apartment: Turkish carpet, lace curtains, the finest of china on marble-top furniture, and chairs beautifully upholstered in velvet, oil paintings and a carved bedstead dressed with a fine feather mattress that would bring good cheer to a man who was to be shot at sunrise. Mr. Kirn owns several farms in Virginia, and the one he lives on has two hundred and seventy acres, and is considered one of the finest in the State.

The next morning the storm had somewhat abated, and I concluded, against the wishes of Mr. Kirn, to continue my trip. I had only gone about a mile when an awful hail-storm came down, and to protect my face I had to cover it with the paddle, and I was blown back to Craney Island, below which I landed and walked again to Mr. Kirn's house, where I was gladly received, and spent another pleasant night. The next morning I started early with the godspeed of Mrs. Kirn and the family, and with a determination to continue my voyage that time at all hazards.

The wind was still high on the eastern shore, and through a chop sea I commenced a trip across the river, which is about three and a half miles wide at this point. When I got out into the channel I found that the tide had not began to ebb as soon as I expected, and before I reached the other shore I was carried back a good distance. That was Sunday, the first of April, and I never will forget it, as I came near being shot twice. Shortly after I reached the western shore (I suppose that is what it is called from the fact that the opposite side is called the eastern shore) and was paddling

in water that was made smoother from rain that
was then falling, I came in sight of some oyster
beds, and saw a little house that was built on piles
for the accommodation of a watchman over the
oyster beds. About that time some large hail-
stones began to fall, and to keep them from striking me in the face I turned and paddled backward.
I afterward ascertained that while I was going
along, head first, the oyster-bed watchman discovered me, and that the day before a large eagle
had flown over his place with a long snake in its
mouth, seeing which the watchman got his gun and
fired at it, wounding the eagle in the wing, which
dropped the snake and flew away. On seeing me,
he said: "There is that d——d eagle again," and
reached for his gun. I fortunately turned around
about that time to see if my course was shaped correctly, when the watchman discovered that it was
a man, and quickly jumped into his boat bare-
headed and pulled toward me for dear life, as the
good fellow thought I was in distress. When he
was near I gave him three blows out of my fog
horn as a salute, which seemed to greatly surprise
him. When he pulled alongside I satisfied his
curiosity by prompt answers to his numerous questions, and accepted an invitation to take a tow to
his cabin, where he assisted me out of the water
and made me welcome to his one-roomed house.
After taking a swig from my flask he told me that
when he was going to shoot me he thought that
my paddle was the eagle's wings, and that the
eagle was trying to pull something out of the water
with its claws. I handed the flask to him and he
kept out the cold by "tipping the rossey" once
more, and the hail having ceased to fall I shook
hands with the good fellow and left him to his
lonely vigil. It was now about five o'clock p. m.,

and I wanted to make Old Point on that tide, which
would last four hours longer. About six o'clock I
reached Sewell's Point, where a number of schooners were in harbor, as the weather was too threaten·
ing and the Roads so rough that it was dangerous
to anchor there. As I reached the point a half rain
and hail storm commenced to pour down, and the
heavy seas from Hampton Roads rolled over me
and made my condition awfully disagreeable. My
hands were numb with the cold, and the small of
my back and feet were chilled through. I saw at
some distance through the storm a large boat with
several men in it put out, and felt confident that
they were coming after me, so I paddled to a spar
buoy that was not far away, and as it had a looped
rope hung to it I put my arm through the loop and
awaited developments. Having my back to the
storm to keep the hail from striking me in the face,
and as the boat was coming that way I did not see
it again until it got quite close. Then to my surprise I found that there were two boats, one with
five men and a gun, and the other had four men.
The fellow with the gun seemed as though he was
disappointed because he did not get a shot at me.
The parties in the other boat came up to me and
insisted on my coming aboard of their schooner
and take something to eat, and I allowed them to
tow me over and they hauled me on the deck of the
"Golden Hind," of Gloucester, Mass., which is
manned by fifteen of as jolly and noble-hearted fellows as ever found harbor in Hampton Roads. They
told me that some hours before they had passed me
in the river on their way from Norfolk; and when I
afterward hove in sight, they watched me as I
neared them until they noticed a fellow put out
from a coaster with a gun in hand. Four of them
then jumped into a " punkey" and pulled for life,

yelling all the while at the other boat not to shoot, and that it was only when the man was taking aim that they succeeded in attracting his attention, which fact was very fortunate for me, as well as for the conscience of the shootist, who must have been a flighty fellow not to have put his glasses on me before taking the chances of a shot. The storm increased every moment, and as it was impossible then for me to cross the Roads, I accepted the pressing invitation of all the crew, who shared the fruits of their labors equally and were all as one, to remain with them for the night, and a very pleasant evening it was. I only regret I did not get all of their names. They were as near Arcadians as any lot of men I have ever met. "There the richest was poor, and the poorest lived in abundance."

Wm. S. Grady, one of the crew, told me he has an uncle, Henry Odlum, who lives at East Boothberry, Maine.

I left the Golden Hind Monday morning at 7 o'clock. The wind was still against the tide, which made a chop sea. But I was now in good sight of my destination, where I landed after four hours of hard work at 11 o'clock. Mr. Phœbus, of the Hygeia Hotel, gave me a hearty welcome, and did all in his power to make my stay with him a pleasant one.

May 4.—I left Cumberland's boat house, in Georgetown, D. C., 7 o'clock in the morning for a swim down the Potomac, and got as far as Fort Foote on the ebb tide, when the tide began to flood. It was then 1 o'clock p. m., and I was fourteen miles down the river from my starting point. The sun was shining very hot, and as I had not anything over my face or eyes, it became very disagreeable, so I landed at the long wharf for a short rest.

On going ashore I walked down the beach to see if I could meet any person, for I was very hungry, and on turning a sharp curve found myself within twenty feet of three colored boys, who had been fishing, and were then sitting on a log eating their lunch. As they had their backs to me I could not withstand the chance that presented itself for a little fun ; so I took my fog-horn in hand, and getting down on all-fours, gave a shrill blow and then commenced jumping toward them. If the devil in his most hideous form had suddenly appeared before those youngsters they could not have been more terrified. Jumping to their feet they ran for life down the beach, where their small boat was fastened, and as two of them jumped into the skiff the third one went head first into the water, and catching hold of the stern of the boat pulled for dear life to get clear of the shore. In the mean time I stood up and was enjoying by a hearty laugh the big scare that my rubber suit had caused, and when the boys had got a reasonable distance from shore they turned to take a more minute scrutiny of what had seemed an awful apparition. When they discovered me standing up with a paddle in hand and laughing, their faces turned from fear to wonder, and in a moment they too commenced smiling, but their teeth chattered like monkeys as they smiled, and it was some time before they could comprehend that I was a real man. Then the two who jumped into the boat in the first scare pretended to have a great joke on the third, who had gone into the cold water, and so it was that they enjoyed what a few moments before seemed to them "his royal majesty the Earl of Hell ;" and I suppose if they live to be a hundred, the impressions formed in that half hour will never leave their memory.

In a few moments I again took to the water, and

after a hot paddle of five hours once more had my
suit removed, to find that my face was so badly
burned that it looked as though it was painted
red, and the next day the skin peeled off.

The articles in the diary are of a miscellaneous
character, relating to many subjects, but they are
of such importance that they cannot fail to interest
the reader. In the writings of the Professor we
find the following admirable article published in a
Boston newspaper :

ALL WOMEN SHOULD SWIM.

There are few subjects of greater interest bearing
on the health of the community than bathing and
swimming, and at this time of the year few topics
of discussion are so constantly referred to by the
newspapers, and our medical contemporaries appear
to treat the matter as of the gravest importance.
Among the multitudes that flock to the various
seaside resorts to spend their holidays, it is somewhat surprising to find that a vast number at each
recurring season content themselves with dawdling
on the beach, inhaling the breezes of the sea, and,
either from timidity or dread of the water, or more
particularly owing to their inability to swim, refrain from even entering the sea, and return after
their holiday year without having at all indulged
in one of the most delightful enjoyments with
which a holiday at the seaside is so pleasurably
associated. This singular timidity attaches itself
even to the sterner sex, though it will be found
prevailing naturally in a wider degree among the
ladies. The first show of the nervous dread of the
water on the part of young boys has been often
overcome by the exemplary prudence and gentle

persuasion of paterfamilias bathing in company
with them, and gradually getting them through
their difficulty by his encouraging presence and
assistance during their "first dip;" and if like
measures were adopted in respect to young girls,
such timidity and nervous apprehensions as we
have before alluded to would doubtless soon disappear, and the healthful exercise of swimming
would be more widely cultivated, and would speedily rank among the most graceful arts and accomplishments of women. At present swimming
among the fair sex seems to be regarded as a most
difficult and dangerous science, whereas experience
shows that it may easily be acquired. There are
certainly many ladies who possess sufficient courage to venture into the sea; but it is amusing to
see them dallying with the rope of the bathing
machine, struggling and splashing in an unsightly
garment that seemingly holds each fair nymph in
bondage, when her limbs should be free and gracefully gliding in healthful exercise through the
freshening water. Owing to the conformation of
the female figure, it is well known to scientists
that an easier flotative power is induced than follows in man, which enables the fair sex to tell us
that "out of a class of thirty girls, whose instruction commenced late last season, twenty-five were
taught to swim in six lessons, and six of them won
prizes;" and during the bathing season at one of
our watering places, it was recorded that three
sisters, wh o were unable to swim, having been carried out by a receding wave, had sufficient presence of mind to turn over on their backs, and in
this position floated safely on shore again. It
remains for some one of enterprise and inventive
powers to design and introduce, for the benefit of
the fair sex especially, some novel and effective

bathing dress, which may enable the art of swimming to be more generally practiced, and to the majority it will then become *un fait accompli*. In the mean time, ladies would do well to bear in mind that anything pressing on the limbs or muscles of the chest interferes with the proper circulation of the blood, and impedes proper progress in the water ; and that perfect freedom for the limbs and body should be recognized as a necessary adjunct to the success of their efforts in the direction of learning to swim. At the various seaside resorts there should be an additional number of bathing machines provided for the accommodation of both ladies and gentlemen, but more particularly in the case of ladies, as we have known instances where ladies having made up their minds for the first venture, on arrival at the beach, finding the few machines engaged have immediately turned back and perhaps never got so far again in overcoming their repugnance to sea bathing. Sea water swimming baths should also be provided in every seaport town ; and they could be made simply by inclosing an area of water with rafts and screens, a grating being fixed on the bottom and sides ; and swimming assistants should be in attendance to give encouragement and instruction to those unaccustomed to the sea-water bath. Ladies' swimming should also be further encouraged in all large towns during the winter by the establishment of tepid swimming baths, with competent teachers—men in preference. Young children should be taught early to swim, and the sooner they are introduced to the water the quicker they will learn to swim, and they will the sooner, perhaps, have the power of saving the lives of their fellow-creatures, should the opportunity occur. It is lamentable to notice the numerous deaths that occur yearly by

4

drowning; and many lives are lost simply because
the agonized spectators are unable to swim, and
therefore cannot venture hand or foot to clutch a
fellow-creature from the grasp of death. If the
art of swimming were more properly understood
and encouraged, it would be a boon to the nation
at large; and in these days of school-board enlight-
enments it would be well if the educators of the
present day would give the question of swimming
some consideration, and extend its benefits to every
school in the country. The cost of a swimming
bath would not be great, and the benefits to be
derived are almost incalculable. Public spirit
is springing up, but the art of swimming is not
followed with that avidity that we should like to
see; and in the interest of the ladies, whose cause
we are now advocating, we hope soon to learn that
among the many graceful accomplishments of the
fair sex the majority of them will be found to excel
in the health-giving exercise of swimming.

Professor Odlum observes that probably not one
in twenty of the persons who indulge in boating on a
holiday can swim. "Nothing," said he, "is more easy.
When the air is out of the body its owner sinks;
when the air is in the body its owner floats. Let
any one slowly draw in his breath as he draws
back his legs and pushes forward his arms, retain
it while he is preparing the stroke which is to pro-
pel him, and slowly allow it to go through his lips
as his arms are passed back from before his head to
his sides and his legs are stretched out. The action
of the stroke should not be quite horizontal, but
should be made on a slight incline downward.
The real reason why people take weeks to learn
how to swim is because swimming professors either

do not know or do not choose to teach the philosophy of breathing, so as to render the body buoyant."

In his diary we find the following sensible remarks: The late frightful disaster on the Sound furnishes another forcible argument for the necessity of acquiring the art of swimming. What a sad commentary on man, whom the Creator endowed with magnificent strength to use his limbs, not to be able to "make an effort," is that furnished by a passenger on the ill-fated Narragansett, who says: "Before rushing on deck to jump overboard I roused several persons, and saw one young man deliberately shoot himself through the head when he realized the danger he was in—not being able to swim." Knowing how to swim or keeping the head above water imparts with it the needed self-reliance and coolness so essential in critical moments.

HYGIENIC SUGGESTIONS.

1. Do not bathe shortly after eating, an interval of an hour and a half should be allowed at least; and do not bathe when tired out, either mentally or physically. Always wait till you feel rested.

2. If overheated when arriving at the bath do not remove your clothes until the excessive feeling of heat has passed, and your breathing and circulation have become regular. Never expose the skin to the direct action of the air when overheated. After resting, a moderate degree of warmth or even perspiration need not prevent your bathing, but do not lounge around the bath undressed.

3. Keep in motion after you have gone into the water; do not stand around chatting and lounging; as soon as you have swum sufficiently, dry your-

self thoroughly, put on your clothes, and keep the blood in circulation by exercise.

4. Do not stay in the water too long. Half an hour is long enough for the strongest man. More delicate persons will find that too much ; for some, ten minutes should be the limit.

5. Ladies should see that their bathing dresses are perfectly dry before using.

6. *Cramp*—Observance of the above rules will most probably prevent the occurrence of cramp. Should a swimmer be seized, however, he should endeavor not to be alarmed, and should strike out vigorously with the affected limb, or, turning on his back, extend it forcibly into the air. By paddling with the hands he can usually reach shore, or keep himself afloat until assistance is rendered.

Swimming is the most useful of all athletic accomplishments, as by it human life is frequently saved. It is also useful in the development of muscular strength, as well as highly beneficial to the nervous system, and often repairs the vital functions falling into decline, and there are few subjects of greater interest bearing on the health of the community than bathing and swimming. Among the multitudes that flock to the various seaside resorts to spend their holidays, it is somewhat surprising to find that a vast number at each recurring season content themselves with dawdling on the beach, inhaling the breezes of the sea, and from dread of the water, *or more particularly owing to their inability to swim,* refrain from ever entering the sea, returning home after their season without having at all indulged in one of the most delightful enjoyments with which a holiday at the seaside is so pleasurably associated.

HINTS TO SWIMMERS.

Captain Webb says:

" When a swimmer is chilled the blood ceases to circulate in the fingers, the finger nails become a deathly white color, the lips turn blue, and should he persist in staying in the water after these symptoms develop he is sure to have cramps. So long as the swimmer can discern spots on his finger nails he knows that his blood is in good order, and that he is safe and free from chills. I have been remarkably free from chills, and feel most at ease when in the salt water under a hot sun. Salt water seems to attract the heat, and, no matter what the temperature of the water, under these circumstances I feel warm. I have on some occasions swam so as to keep my body under water, but even in such instances on coming out I have found my back and limbs blistered. This shows the penetration of the heat from the rays of the sun on the water. On one occasion since I was here last I swam for £400 at Scarborough, staying in the water seventy-four hours. I use a preparation of porpoise oil, which I rub all over my body, even my face. The oil fills up the pores of the skin and keeps the salt water from penetrating my vitals."

PHYSICAL CULTURE.

It is a well-authenticated fact that the American people in the last twenty years have degenerated physically more than any other nation, unless possibly the French.

The causes and reasons for this degeneracy are obvious.

They have become the most prosperous nation

upon the face of the earth.   They are essentially a
money-making people, and not a few individuals
in private life have accumulated fortunes equal to
a prince's-possessions.

This has reacted in two ways to their physical
detriment.   Those who have already become
wealthy have settled down into habits of indolence
and ease, "doing nothing with masterly inactivity,"
while those still engaged in accumulating wealth
have allowed themselves to become slaves to their
commercial pursuits or professions, and in both
cases are dwindling gradually into an *effete* race
of people.

Most of the so-called modern conveniences of a
higher civilization conduce, directly or indirectly,
toward the evil that threatens them, and indulging
in a street-car ride or yielding to the luxury of a
close carriage, when they should walk home after
a day spent in an office or counting-room, fosters
and encourages this evil in an alarming degree.
On the growing population we see the effects of
this luxuriant self-indulgence and the neglect of
physical training most painfully marked.   So much
so has this become a fact that a school boy or girl
of splendid physique is very seldom seen.

The cramming process of competitive examina-
tions, to which budding manhood and womanhood
are now subjected, combined with the total lack of
physical discipline, another injudicious diet demanded by a capricious appetite, is creating not a
race of intellectual giants but of corporeal pigmies.

Well directed gymnastic exercise tends to the
growth and development of man, favors the preser-
vation of general health by calling into direct action a majority of the vital organs of the body.   It
also acts powerfully upon the skin by stimulating
the pores, through which a vast proportion of the

waste matter of the system is carried off. Exercise is likewise important in order to fortify the body against the attacks of unhealthy influences, for it is a well-known fact, admitted by the highest authority, that neither typhoid fever, diphtheria or any other of the infectious diseases can be so readily imbibed into the system where the several organs of the body are in full energy and vigor.

Sedentary habits are the fruitful source of manifold disease; they produce indigestion and dyspepsia, the utmost degree of physical wretchedness; from these spring nearly " all the ills that flesh is heir to." City life exhibits no more pitiful phase than the pale-faced men with attenuated bodies who perform the clerical duties of the Government departments or the mental labor of the community, and it is to benefit such as these who may be seen on our streets by thousands that human intelligence, enlightened by science, recommends the gymnasium. A system of gentle exercise is here provided which calls every muscle into play and distributes the circulation to the utmost and minute fibers, thus infusing a generous glow and imparting a tonic which no artificial stimulus can vie with in flavor or effect. If such a thing as perfect health is possible in city life, it is found in the healthful systematic exercise in the gymnasium and bathing. It is well understood that gymnasts enjoy the very act of living, that they are free from the aches and pains common to the majority of men of sedentary habits, yet their condition is attainable by all.

A sound mind in a sound body is the grandest possession mortals can have—better than power or position. Which is the way to get both and keep them? Good education, moral and intellectual, serves for the one; good air, temperate living and

healthful exercise serve for the other.   One of the
first and most important propositions is to har-
monize the conditions of life and business duties
with public health.   Any one who promotes this
harmony is a public benefactor.   Hygienic science
has discovered that disease even may be cured, and
that the debilitating effects of special occupations
may be counteracted by the judicious use of particular exercise.

For these reasons in-door gymnastic and muscular exercises have become to be an institution not
only for the invalid but for all ; and especially for
persons of sedentary occupation this is found invaluable.   If simply walking up and down a room is
relief after protracted desk work, how much more
beneficial is a change of muscular action ?   And
after long stooping, a change by which the back
muscles are brought into use is a positive rest.

A popular hygienist says that one-half the people
in civilized life are either born or become imperfect
in some part of the body.   This is true enough.
It is equally true that this may be remedied by
proper training.

Systematic and healthful exercise consists in frequent changes in the position of the body, bring-
ing into action at every change a different set of
muscles, thereby strengthening and symmetrically
developing every part of the body.   Thus exercise
may become an exhilarating pleasure instead of a
tiresome and exhausting labor.   By using light
weights at first and frequent changing the movements, the weight and movement of exercise can
be gradually increased without fatigue.

Physical training is as important to the body as
culture is to the mind.   Bodily strength may be
present and the individual be unable to use that
strength with any degree of success.   It requires

a trained hand to make a barrel or a boot, and it requires a trained mind to exhibit the highest success in the arrangement and expression of thoughts and in the successful management of business. A person may have an educated mind in reference to music, and yet not have the trained hand necessary to play the piano forte. But when the hand is trained to perform the dictates of the will, and the mind is also educated in musical science, the mere sights of the notes will send the hands to the requisite keys almost instinctively. Such is physical training. The expert swimmer is as much at home on the wave as on the land. He delights in the watery element, while the effeminate will view the water with feelings akin to terror. The men and women of England will walk miles before breakfast, and the glow—the ruddy glow of health that distinguishes them—will show that exercise is the best of all medicines. The women of Germany, yoked by the side of dogs to draw heavy loads, are the pictures of health and good nature. Certainly the most striking character which arrests the attention of the traveler in his first rambles about Stockholm is the Dalecarlian boatwomen. Let him walk in whatever direction he may, if his path leads him to cross any of the numerous arms of the sea or of the Malar, he is sure to find his boat manned by peasant women with stalwart frames and brawny muscular arms, and faces more remarkable for good nature than for beauty, looking out from a close-fitting cap of peculiar form. So strongly formed are these women that they seem more calculated to afford protection than to stand in need of it from the sex ordinarily acknowledged to be the lords of creation. I know not as yet what may be the appearance of the masculine portion of the people of this province, but if the hand of the

Creator has not endowed them with truly herculean frames, I think they must stand a poor chance with their amazonian *better halves*.

Thus we see in all countries that where the inhabitants take exercise or have a tendency to physical culture, the men are strong and athletic, and the women wear the bloom of health, if not of beauty, upon their cheeks. Disease is of rare occurrence, and they can realize the truth of the old adage "that health is greater than wealth;" in fact the greatest of all earthly blessings, for without it the richest man is poor indeed.

MALARIA.

There is no word that is more thoroughly incorporated with the speech and thought of the people than malaria. It has become a convenient resource for ignorance, although it is invariably coupled with wisdom and its utterances. It is the familiar designation of many diseases for which no other name or explanation is available. It is the one thing to be avoided in all changes of residence, and it is the dark pall that hangs over some districts of our country, and will be found on investigation that the people have only themselves to blame; that they have entirely overlooked all sanitary laws, and that malaria in their case means imperfect drainage, overflowing cesspools, the use of water from filthy wells, and decayed vegetable and animal matter accumulated in the streets and on private premises.

Malaria simply means bad air, which is the source of disease, and not disease itself. The seeds of a complaint may be in the system, the result of imperfect nutrition or of vitiated blood, and a bad atmosphere may develop the fever or bring a con-

gestive chill quickly to the surface, but the mis-
fortunes occur at all times and in all places; only
appearing in isolated cases and as the result of
well-known causes, they are not classed in the
usual column, at least by sensible physicians. Yet,
the patient and friends are happy in thinking that
they have the whole thing in a nutshell; it is, in
a word, malaria. And especially is there a kind
of grim comfort to the semi-invalids, to those who
are by no means sick, yet not entirely well. They
have some flying aches and pains, a little head-
ache, a loss of appetite, and they feel a little
feverish. It is nothing, only a little malaria. There
is both good and evil in these distempered fancies:
good when the fear of malarious influences leads
to those precautions really necessary to health, and
evil when the imagination becomes diseased and
every locality teems with fever and kindred com-
plaints. It is quite as much a malarious disease as
any other. If not generated by a bad atmosphere,
it is certainly transmitted from one to another by
it, and all predisposing symptoms are thereby
heightened and developed. The "cleanliness that
is next to godliness" is the great essential in this
and many other visitations. Air may be naturally
bad, the product of swamps, of marshes, and of de-
caying vegetable matter, but we can create an atmosphere in cities far worse than any to be encoun-
tered in the country.

The air of tenement houses, back yards with its
cesspools and other abominations, or even that of
the sick rooms, often unventilated for days and
weeks, produces the worst form of malaria.

EFFECT OF MARSHES IN PRODUCING FEVER.

Warden, in his account of the United States of

America, remarks : " All low parts of the United States along the banks of rivers and lakes, and near the borders of stagnant waters and in marshy situations, where vegetable or animal substances, in a state of decay, are exposed to the action of the autumnal sun, are subject to an intermittent or bilious fever. In every low situation, where the rich vegetable soil is first exposed to the action of the sun, or where the water disappearing presents to its action a muddy surface, deleterious emanations are produced, which, ascending to the surface of a neighboring hill, become the cause of disease there, as well as near the surface where they originated."

He gives a great number of instances of fevers having broken out in America in the neighborhood of marshes ; and he also cites from various authors cases showing the pestilential effect of marshes in Europe on the health. The Pontine marshes in Italy are well known to have produced for centuries numerous febrile diseases. Lancisit, physician to Pope Clement XI, relates that in the vicinity of Rome thirty persons of both sexes, and of the highest rank, being on a party of pleasure near the mouth of the Tiber, the wind suddenly changed, and blew from the south across putrid marshes ; and that such was its effect that all except one were suddenly seized with tertian fever. An inundation of the rivers of Hungary, which covered many parts of the country with stagnant water, is said to have occasioned the loss of 40,000 of the Austrian army. The annual overflow of the Nile has produced the same effect, from the earliest times, at Alexandria and other places.

In August, 1765, a continued or remitting fever was produced among the soldiers and marines stationed in the island of Portsea, in the neighborhood of stagnant waters, and a great number of them were carried off.

Warden remarks that "the most extraordinary fact regarding marsh miasmas is that their influence is more sensibly on the summits of the neighboring hills than on the very borders of the marsh whence they emanate. An invisible and pestiferous vapor, which rises by its lightness, or is wafted by currents of air, hovers on the summit during the hot season, and soon paralyzes the strongest constitutions."

He gives several instances where such pestilential exhalations have produced fevers at the distance of two miles. The short duration of human life in marshy districts has been remarked by all writers on population. For example, the average duration of life is at least one-third lower in Holland than in England or France. In Switzerland, according to the observations of Muret, the probability of life, or the age to which half the born live, was as follows: In nine parishes of the Alps, 47 years; in 41 parishes of the Paysde Vaud and Jura, 42; in 12 parishes where grain was cultivated, 40; in 18 parishes among the great vineyards, 37; *in one marshy parish, 24!*

I know by personal experience that such is the case among the marshes and along the shores of the Chesapeake. I contracted malaria at Lower Cedar Point, and contracted more while at the Hygeia Hotel, Fortress Monroe, and it is still in my system. I never expect to be the same man physically again. I have expended a great deal of money to get relief, but have failed. I never knew what an hour's sickness was previous to my contracting malaria.

THE WONDERS OF THE DEEP.

Very few persons, even among those who delight
in studying other branches of natural history, are
acquainted with the wonders of the deep. I have
always taken an especial interest in the subject, and
have often thought while taking my long swims on
the surface of the water that I should like to explore
the caverns of the ocean, not alone for the treasures
they contained, gone down with the wrecks of by-
gone storms, with chests of gold, and doomed to
molder away beyond the reach of avaricious man,
but to see the curiosities and monstrosities of the
deep—the monsters and fishes—that no one has
ever seen or described. The various phenomena
and the inhabitants of the water are not only
quite as well worthy our investigation as those of
the dry land, but being less familiar from coming
under personal observation less frequently, they
present far greater novelty, and their variety is
inexhaustible.

Fishes, or, as they have been fancifully called,
"the birds of the sea," occupy an important place
in the animal kingdom. Their classification is
simple: they are distinguished from other ver-
tebrate animals by their modes of respiration; they
have gills instead of lungs, and they are distinguished from the crustacea by having no backbone.

I have heard of a story of a person who, studying
the natural history of fishes, wrote to a friend asking him to collect specimens for him. "I shall be
delighted to do so," was the reply, "and shall send
you all I can catch, from a whale to a shrimp." A
very little acquaintance would have shown him that
neither of these are fish; and a little knowledge
would not in this case have been so "dangerous a

thing'' as it is sometimes supposed by the idle and ignorant.

The contrast and analogy between fishes and the aerial tribes are very curious and interesting. Both are fitted to move in a fluid medium—in an ocean of their own. The bird swims in the air, as the fish may be said to fly in the water, by similar though not the same means. The feathers of one are analogous to the scales of the other; the wings to the pectoral fins, and the tail of both acts the part of a rudder. Many persons have thought that the movements of the aquatic animal are more graceful and elegant than those of the aerial, in consequence of the greater flexibility of its form and the number of its motive organs. Perhaps our own predilections may be in favor of the feathered race, because we regard them as the friends of our childhood; but undoubtedly there is considerable grace and beauty in the agile movements of fishes, especially in their own pure element, which they rarely though occasionally forsake. The proverbial expression, "a fish out of water," gives a lively idea of a "false position." The instances in which it actually occurs are well worthy our notice.

Dr. Hancock mentions a fish (the loricaria) which creeps upon all-fours in the beds of rivers. This little finny quadruped has a very singular appearance moving upon its four stilts, which are produced by a bony ray in front of its pectoral fins and of the next pair to them. The callicthys, a Brazilian fish, walks in this way for miles in search of water when, as often happens, the pool in which it lives dries up.

The climbing perch (perca scandens) not only creeps along the shore, but ascends trees in search of the crustacea upon which it feeds. It is found in Tranquebar. It must have some difficulty in ascending the fan-palms if it were not provided with numerous little spines or thorns upon its fins, by means of which it suspends itself while climbing, using them like hands.

In addition to these peculiarities, it has the power of folding up both dorsal and anal fins when not using them, and thus it literally puts its hands in its pockets; for it deposits them in a cavity in its body, provided by nature on purpose to receive them when they are not needed for progression. Nor are these pockets or troughs peculiar to the climbing perch; the land crabs also possess them. With respect to the latter, anatomists were formerly puzzled to account for the fact of animals whose mode of respiration is by gills, being able to exist so long out of water without injury to those organs, but a French naturalists first, and afterward Milne Edwards, discovered a cavity or trough into which a small quantity of water is kept in order to moisten their gills occasionally. The gecarcinusuca, one species of this tribe, has more than one pocket or vesicle for that purpose; another species, the orypode, has a different but equally curious apparatus, a small spongy substance, by means of which the animal is supplied with the moisture required. The reason of this remarkable adaptation is fraught with instruction and interest, and it is a beautiful example of the unbroken order and exquisite harmony which pervade all the works of the Divine Author of the universe. Kirby remarks that God, when he created these tribes, would not separate them from their kind by giving them a different mode of respiration, but provided this compensating contrivance to fit them for the circumstances in which He decreed to place them.

The perca scandens is not the only kind of fish which ascends trees in search of food. Several species are found in the Polynesian Islands climbing the cocoa-palms; the most remarkable of them is a kind of lobster of gigantic size, and of strength sufficient to open the cocoa-nuts upon which it chiefly subsists.

Nor are these the only instances of the inhabitants of the waters forsaking their native element. Several varieties of fish in the Indian Ocean and in the Mediterranean are adapted to a short flight, and these peculiarities of habit and movement are highly interesting, even were they devoid of gracefulness; for they are examples of a contrivance which displays the goodness of the Creator in furnishing them with the means of providing for themselves amid the accidents and difficulties that may fall to their lot.

Fishes have the character of being remarkably stupid, and yet they are not wholly incapable of instruction. In many parts of Germany the trout, carp and tench are summoned to their food by the sound of a bell; and in the gardens of the Tuileries some fish were kept for more than a century which would come when called by their names. Neither are they as wholly deficient in parental instinct as has generally been supposed. Two species of fish in Brazil, one the calicthys, before mentioned, the other called doras, construct actual nests—the former of grass, the latter of leaves—in which they deposit their eggs, covering them very carefully. They live in Paris, and, like birds, watch and defend their nests by turns till their young are hatched and able to take care of themselves.

A similar instinct is exhibited by a fish resembling the turbot, osphromenus olfax, which is kept for food in ponds in the Mauritius. After making their nest and laying their eggs, the male and female hatch and watch their offspring by turns.

5

The quiet and seclusion of a pond or some such quiet retreat are indispensable to the development of this parental instinct, and accordingly the inhabitants of the great world of waters exhibit no traces of it.

The longevity of fish is another remarkable circumstance considered with regard to their constant exposure to injury, and the soft, defenseless nature of their conformation.

In the year 1754, an old pike in a pond belonging to the castle of Kaisenslantern had a ring in his gill with an inscription stating that it had been put there in 1487, two hundred and sixty-seven years before, by order of the Emperor Frederic II. It weighed three hundred and fifty pounds. Knowing the predaceous and remorseless habits of this fresh-water shark, we feel assured it was a monster of rapacity, and no doubt the scourge and terror of the pond in which it reigned as tyrant. The existence of such relentless destroyers is, however, of absolute necessity to check the redundant increase of the finny tribes ; for the cod alone produces more than nine millions of eggs in a year, and if neither man nor shark made it their food the sea would in a short time contain nothing but cod-fish. It has, therefore, been wisely ordered that the larger species should swallow the small fry by hundreds at a time ; they in turn feed upon their minuter brethren, and even the herbivorous ones breakfast upon the eggs of fishes.

The adaptation of fishes to the circumstances in which they are placed affords a most interesting subject of inquiry ; this variety of form appears inexhaustible, and it is thought that the sea contains the analogous of almost every aerial or terrestrial race. The monsters of the deep are undoubtedly more gigantic and grotesque than any of their representatives on land. Among the former, the whale, though not a fish, claims pre-eminence as regards magnitude. Its value and usefulness, in a commercial point of view, are so well known that we are apt to forget how wonderful it is ; that the huge leviathan should be subservient to man, ministering in various ways to his comfort and luxury.

Among marine giants we must not overlook the sun-fish, or mola, with its enormous phosphorescent carcass, shining with a brightness like the reflection of the moon in the water, and measuring twenty-five feet in length. Imagine a party of them (they generally travel five or six together) on a dark, moonless night, frightening the rest of the fish, scaring the superstitious sailor, and astonishing even the veteran naturalist who has left off being surprised at anything.

Next in bulk comes the " requin," which is thought to be identical with the carcharias of the Greeks, mistranslated the whale, in the history of Jonah.

The next in size is the "sqalus maximus," sometimes more than forty feet in length, to say nothing of the enormous ray-fish, one of which, taken at Barbadoes, required seven pair of oxen to draw it on shore.

The sailors call it the sea-devil, and naturalists describe it as frightful. But all these are " gentle monsters " compared with the horrible and terrific octopods, the hideousness of which far surpasses anything that imagination could have pictured.

But if tired of considering mere bulk and deformity, let us turn for variety to the " treasures of the deep," to the beautiful tribe of shells, the corallines, the sea flowers, and the ocean beds of weeds on which the gregarious fishes graze like land animals in their pastures.

Let us contemplate the connecting links between animal and vegetable life ; let us consider the electric fishes from the torpedo and gymnotus down to the aquatic stars which beautify the nights of tropical climates ; let us admire the migratory instinct which at their appointed seasons collects such vast numbers of edible fish, and brings them within the reach of man for his food or convenience ; we shall then begin to have some idea how inexhaustible is the interest of the subject, and when we consider how wonderful are the works of the Almighty Creator, shall be constrained to proclaim, "In wisdom hast Thou made them all ; the earth is full of Thy riches." To which I may add, so is the great deep also—the wide and fathomless deep.

THE SEAMAN.

In reference to sea-faring there is, in the minds of most persons, a wild, romantic idea. Poets have sung of the sea—of its might and its mystery ; of its silence and its storms ; of its beauty and its wrath. When the seaman quits the land and trusts his life and fortunes upon the bosom of the deep, and has only the vaulted sky and the planets and stars as subjects of permanency and trust, he is hidden, buried, as it were, from all his friends and associations. For months, and, perhaps, years no word reaches his friends as to his safety, and some, alas ! are never heard of more. Their death and the place of their sepulture is a mystery forever.

In connection with all that relates to the sea there is uncertainty and mystery, and it is not strange that the stoutest-hearted seamen entertain feelings of superstitious fear relative to special days, unlucky ships, the appearance of birds and other omens of good and ill. Some of Dana's "Three Years before the Mast" and Captain Maryatt's sea stories have been read by boys with more enthusiasm than any thing else.

The seaman is required to have physical courage, prudence and bodily vigor and endurance; he should have intellectual capabilities and a good degree of culture. There is no reason why seamen should be proverbially rough, base, outcast men. True, in large cities there are many temptations to vice and demoralization, and some men, who are seamen, ran away from home before their characters were formed and fell into bad company and bad habits; yet there are many quiet citizen-seamen who are at home rejoicing with their families as sober Christian men, saving their wages and building up an enviable prosperity. On a Sunday their brown faces, with the wife and group of pretty children, may be seen in the pews of the churches. The best young men learn the science of the sea, and honor the profession they follow. In the large commercial towns the veterans of the sea—the victims of land sharks and intemperance—may haunt the public imagination, but there is no reason why men of culture and first-class talent and morals, like Nelson and Porter and Farragut, should not be common in this great field of industry. Every seaman should understand the science of navigation, for every officer might be stricken down or washed overboard in a storm, and it would be desirable if each seaman were able to take the ship's papers and work her voyage half around the world. This was once the case with a large East India ship which lost every officer by cholera, when the captain's wife, Mrs. Blount, understanding navigation, brought the noble ship home to Southampton, England, about the year 1850.

The heroic conduct of Mrs. Mary A. Patten, aged twenty years, wife of Capt. Joshua Patten, of Boston, must be remembered with pleasure and pride by many. They sailed from New York in July, 1856, for San Francisco in the clipper ship Neptune's Car. When doubling Cape Horn, the captain suspended the mate for neglect of duty, and had double duty to perform ; becoming ill of brain fever, Mrs. Patten, understanding navigation, nursed her delirious husband and took the ship in safety to San Francisco. The underwriters of New York presented her with a purse of a thousand dollars.

During the late war some of the bravest battles were fought and won by the jolly tars of the sea. The life of the common seaman is necessarily a hard one. Exposed to all kinds of weather, cooped up within the narrow confines of a ship, deprived of the comforts of home and friends, they, taken as a class, deserve rather the commendation than the condemnation of mankind. They man the ships that fight our battles on the high seas, they carry our flag into every port of the world, they have made our country respected in every land. They come back to their native land in great ships laden with the products and luxuries of other climes, and they stand as the bulwark of the nation's honor when our dominion is disputed on the great oceans that wash our shores. Too much honor cannot be given the jolly tars, and their comfort, their education and their well being should engage the attention of us all.

Reference has been made in a former chapter to the fondness of the Patagonians for swimming and what estimate they attach to the knowledge of that art. It is only necessary to quote a description of this race of giants to show the benefit derived from

physical culture. Find a person fond of athletic
sports and we will show you a healthy frame possessing a robust constitution free from the common
ills that afflict mankind :

"The Patagonians, whom some travelers have
magnified into giants, are really somewhat larger
than Europeans. With an average height rather
exceeding six feet, they have very broad shoulders
and a large head, the ample dimensions of which
are set off by a quantity of long matted hair hang-
ing in the wildest disorder over their faces. Falkner, who lived many years among the Patagonians,
says that he never saw one of them who was above
an inch or two taller than Cacique Cangapol ; and
' he,' observes the Jesuit, ' must have been seven
feet and some inches in height, because on tiptoe I
could not reach the top of his head.'

"The exaggerations of those who have repre-
sented the Patagonians as a race of giants, eight
feet in height and with the voice of bulls, are, after
all, less embarrassing than the silence of others
respecting the superior stature of the natives inhabit-
ing the northern shores of the Strait of Magalhaens.
But it must be observed that these people are
great wanderers, roving over an immense extent
of desert plains.

"The same tribe, which was found by the officers
of the Beagle on the shores of the strait, was seen
a year after on the banks of the Rio Negro, eight
hundred miles further north. It is probable, also,
that the various tribes differ in robustness according to the abundance of their food ; and, indeed,
Falkner points out the distinction between the
large-bodied and the small Huilliches. This circumstance, added to their nomadic habits, will
serve to explain why it has not been the lot of every

visitor to the Magellanic shores to see natives with the herculean proportions of Cangapol.

INHABITANTS OF TIERRA DEL FUEGO.

" The inhabitants of Tierra del Fuego have but little temptation to cultivate the soil ; their solid and habitable land is reduced to the stony beach on which they wander in quest of food ; and, owing to the steepness of the coast, they can only move about in their canoes. These are made of branches intertwined and covered with bark ; and, though small and frail, the natives are not afraid to venture in them a considerable distance from the shore, and even to hoist a sail of sealskin. The canoe is plastered inside with clay, and in the middle of it a fire is kept burning ; yet the Fuegian, in this case attentive to his comfort, appears in general insensible to cold.

" The women dive for sea-eggs in winter as well as summer ; a small skin thrown over the shoulders or round the loins constitutes the whole clothing of either sex ; and their naked limbs are protected from the sharp winds only by being smeared with clay. Their shores supply them with seals and various kinds of shell-fish ; with their slings and arrows they are able to kill sea-fowl even on the wing. In the art of fishing they appear to have made little progress. An old voyager relates that on his hauling a net eighty feet long in' the Strait of Magelhaens, the natives, previously on friendly terms with him, grew so incensed at the great quantity of fish thus taken at once that they immediately commenced an assault on him with stones."

While aboard of a steamer on the Chesapeake, some time ago, I had frequent questions asked me

in relation to the gulls and other fowl that skim
over the surface of the water.   I answered every
question as best I could under the circumstances,
(having but little time to do so,) but afterward, as
a result of the questioning, I gave my attention to
the subject and sought information respecting those
birds that flap their broad wings over the wave and
are rocked to sleep on the crest of the billow.   There
are birds of good and ill omen.   Among the latter
is the—

STORMY PETREL.

This ominous harbinger of the deep is seen nearly
throughout the whole expanse of the Atlantic from
Newfoundland to the tropical parts of America,
whence it wanders even to Africa and the coasts of
Spain.   From the ignorance and superstition of
mariners an unfavorable prejudice has long been
entertained against these adventurers and harmless
wanderers, and as sinister messengers of the storm,
in which they are often involved with the vessel
they follow, they have been unjustly stigmatized
by the name of Stormy Petrels, Devil's Birds and
Mother Carey's Chickens.   At nearly all seasons
of the year these swallow petrels in small flocks are
seen wandering almost alone over the wide waste
of the ocean.
On the edge of soundings, as she loses sight of
the distant head-land, and launches into the depths
of the unbounded and fearful abyss of waters, flocks
of these dark, swift-flying and ominous birds begin
to shoot around the vessel, and finally take their
station in her foaming wake.   In this situation, as
humble dependents, they follow for their pittance
of fare, constantly and keenly watching the agitated surge for any floating mollusca, and are ex-
tremely gratified with any kind of fat animal matter

thrown overboard, which they invariably discover, however small the morsel or mountainous and foaming the raging wave on which it may happen to float. On making such discovery they suddenly stop in their airy and swallow-like flight, and whirl instantly down to the water. Sometimes nine or ten thus crowd together like a flock of chickens scrambling for the same morsel ; at the same time pattering on the water with their feet, as if walking on the surface. They balance themselves with gently fluttering and outspread wings, and often dip down their heads to collect the sinking object in pursuit. On other occasions, as if seeking relief from their almost perpetual exercise of flight, they jerk and hop widely over the water, rebounding as their feet touches the surface with great agility and alertness.

There is something cheerful and amusing in the sight of these little flocks, steadily following after the vessel, so light and unconcerned across the dreary ocean. During a gale it is truly interesting to witness their intrepidity and address. Unappalled by the storm that strikes terror into the breast of the mariner, they are seen coursing wildly and rapidly over the waves, descending their sides, then mounting with the breaking surge which threatens to burst over their heads, sweeping through the hollow waves as in a sheltered valley, and again mounting with the rising billow, it trips and jerks sportively and securely on the surface of the roughest sea, defying the horrors of the storm, and like some magic being seems to take delight in braving overwhelming dangers. At other times we see these aerial messengers playfully coursing from side to side in the wake of the ship, making excursions far and wide on every side, now in advance, then far behind, returning again to the vessel, as if she were stationary, though moving at the most rapid rate. A little after dark they generally cease their arduous course, and take their uninterrupted rest upon the water, arriving in the wake of the vessel they have left, as I have observed, by about nine or ten o'clock of the following morning. In this way we were followed by the same flock of birds.

According to Buffon, the petrel acquires its name from the Apostle Peter, who is also said to have walked upon the water. At times we hear from these otherwise silent birds by day, a low *weet, weet*, and in the craving anxiety, apparently to obtain something from us, they utter a low twittering *pe up* or chirp. In the night, when disturbed by the passage of the vessel, they rise in a low, vague and hurried flight from the water, and utter a singular guttural chattering, like, *kuk, kuk, k' k' k' k' k' k'* or something similar, ending in a low twitter like that of the swallow.

These petrels are said to breed in great numbers on the rocky shores of the Bahama Islands and the Bermuda, and along some parts of the coast of east Florida and Cuba. I am informed that they also breed in large flocks on the mud and sand islands off Cape Sable, in Nova Scotia, burrowing downward from the surface to the depth of a foot or more. They also commonly employ the holes and cavities of rocks near the sea for this purpose. After the period of incubation they return to feed their young only during the night, with oily food which they raise from their stomachs. At these times they are heard through most parts of the night, making a continual cluttering sound like frogs. In June and July, or about the time that they breed, they are still seen out at sea for scores of leagues from the land, the swiftness of their flight allowing them daily to make these vast excursions in quest of their ordinary prey ; and hence besides their suspicious appearance in braving storms, as if aided by the dark ruler of the air, they breed, according to the vulgar opinion of sailors, like no other honest bird ; for taking no time for the purpose on land, they merely hatch their egg, it is said, under their wings as they sit on the water.

The food of this species appears to consist of gelatinous spora of the Gulf weed, as well as small fish, barnacles and probably many small mollusca. Their flesh is rank, oily and unpleasant to the taste.

The petrel is about six and three-fourths inches in length ; the alar extent being about thirteen and a half. The bill black ; head black, and lower parts brownish black ; greater wing coverts pale brown, minutely tipped with white ; wings and tail black ; legs and naked parts of the thighs black, slight rudiment of a hind toe. The membrane of the foot is marked with a spot of straw yellow, and finally serrated along the edges. Iridis dark brown.

GENIUS.

There is no one possession or quality so highly estimated or so valuable as this ; other qualities, a cultivated mind, a moral tone of character, etc., are justly prized, and the possessor of any of them is respected, and exercises a commensurate influence. But even these qualities are shadowed, as by a dark cloud, in comparison with genius. No simile can correctly describe genius. The reverence one has for it is not unlike the sensation experienced when, in solitude, we gaze on the waters of the Niagara falling into its dread abyss, and harken to the voice of the terror-stricken river, awful as the roar of a multitude of lions. The awe one feels may be likened to that which creeps o'er the mind of the intellectual traveler, as, in the valley of Chamouni, he turns his gaze to the snowy dome of that monarch of the Alps, Mont Blanc. Far towering beyond the summits of that lofty range rises that giant form. But seldom has human foot trod on the holy spot; there, too often, has death joined the adventurous band that has attempted it—so high, so vast, so unapproachable, it seems fit for the throne of the Eternal. The deep breathing of nature, the sounds of muttering thunder, heard with fearful distinctness in that still moment which immediately precedes the storm, convey to the mind sensations not unlike those awakened by the sight of genius.

And yet the possessor of it, this priceless, this inestimable gift, passes among his fellows—the man who had stirred the spirit of a nation, whose words have been inlaid in the monuments of national fame and greatness, moves among his kind scarce noticed; the vulgar, the rough, the uncouth rub against him. It is as if the fish-fag should jostle the graceful person of some creature of light and beauty. Ottway died of want. 'Tis told of him that, pressed by hunger, he actually broke into a coffee-room in London, and seized a loaf of bread on a table! The divine Milton was poor; and Shakspeare, the incomparable, he was talked of in his day by some dogmatic magistrate as "one William Shakspeare." A baronet, one Lucy, caused him to be apprehended as a deer-stalker.

Into what utter, entire, unspeakable, insignificance sink wealth and rank and title when compared to genius, as is here exemplified in the appreciation of the two individuals now referred to—Lucy, the great man of his country, the baronet or lord,

and Shakspeare! Hyperion to the Satyr, indeed.
We think of one as a laden vessel, an earthen por-
ringer; of the other as a jeweled cup. Genius is
sure to be appreciated by posterity; but then posterity does not minister to the comfort of the physical man. It is a rare treat to see a man of genius
petitioning the rich man or soliciting the influence
of an official. It is as if the monarch of the woods
should entreat the wise-looking Jocko! And yet
how often is the sight seen. 'Tis pitiful, 'tis laugh-
able, 'tis painful. Merriment and indignation
go hand in hand together as we contemplate such
a scene.

Pilgrims visit Mecca's shrine—the sepulcher.
Religion beckons them to the holy spot. So do fame
and honor beckon to the tombs of the sons of genius
generation after generation of men. The soil
around them is sacred; one treads softly as if he
were intruding; he scrapes together some of the
earth, and bears it away to his distant land.

EARLY ASSOCIATIONS.

The scenery amidst which we are born and
brought up, if we remain long enough therein to
have passed that early period of existence on which
memory seems to have no hold, sinks, as it were,
into the spirit of man, twines itself intimately with
every thought, and becomes a part of his being. He
can never cast it off any more than he can cast off
the body in which the spirit acts. Almost every
chain of his after-thoughts is linked at some point
to the magical circle which bounds his youth's
ideas; and even when latent, and in no degree
known, it is still present, affecting every feeling
and every fancy, and giving a bent of its own to all
our words and our deeds.   *   *   *   The passing

of our days may be painful, the early years may be checkered with grief and care, unkindness and frowns may wither the smiles of boyhood, and tears bedew the path of youth ; yet, nevertheless, when we stand and look back in later life, letting memory hover over the past, prepared to light where she will, there is no period in all the space laid out before her over which her wings flutter so joyfully, or on which she would so much wish to pause, as the times of our youth. The evils of other days are forgotten, the scenes in which those days passed are remembered, detached from the sorrows that checkered them, and the bright misty light of life's first sunrise still gilds the whole with glory not its own.

BODILY AND MENTAL EVILS.

It is a terrible thing when youth—the time of sport and enjoyment, the period which nature has set apart for acquiring knowledge and power and expansion, and for tasting all the multitude of sweet and magnificent things which crowd the creation in their first freshness and with the zest of novelty, is clouded with storms or drenched with tears. It is not so terrible by any means when the mere ills of fortune afflict us ; for they are light things to the buoyancy of youth, and are soon thrown off by the heart which has not learned the foresight of fresh sorrows. The body habituates itself more easily to anything than the mind, and privations twice or thrice endured are privations no longer. But it is a terrible thing, indeed, when, in those warm days of youth when the heart is all affection, the mind longing for thrilling sympathies, the soul eager to love and be loved, the faults, the vices, or the circumstances of others, cut us off from

those sweet natural ties with which nature, as with
a wreath of flowers, has garlanded our early days;
when we have either lost and regret or known but
to condemn, the kindred whose veins flow with the
same blood as our own, or the parents who gave
us being.

SUBMARINE BALLOON SERVICE.

Knowing the interest I take in such subjects, a
friend of mine, an officer in the United States
Navy, writes me as follows from Europe:

"The International Exhibition of Nice is reserv-
ing some wonders for the foreigners who may propose to pass a portion of the winter of 1883–'84
upon the borders of Mediterranean.

"One of these wonders is a balloon which its
inventor, Mr. Toselli, calls "the observatory under
the sea." It is made of steel and bronze, to enable
it to resist the pressure which the water produces at
a depth of one hundred and twenty meters. This
"observatory under the sea" has a height of eight
meters, and is divided into three compartments.

"The upper apartment is reserved for the commander, to enable him to direct and watch the
working of the observatory, and to give to the passengers the explanations necessary as to the depth
of the sea.

"The second apartment, in the center of the
machine, is comfortably furnished for passengers
to the number of eight, who are placed so that they
can see a long distance from the machine. They
have under their feet a glass which enables them
to examine at their ease the bottom of the sea, with
its fishes, its plants, and its rocks.

"The obscurity being almost complete at seventy
meters of depth, the observatory will be provided

with a powerful electric sun, which sheds light to a great distance in lighting these depths. They have at their disposal a telephone, which allows them to converse with their friends who have stopped on the steamboat which transports the voyagers to such places as are known as the most curious in the neighborhood. They have also a handy telegraph machine. Beneath the passengers an apartment is reserved for the machine, which is constructed on natural principles ; that is to say, as the vessel of a fish, becoming heavier or lighter at command, so as to enable the machine to sink or rise at the wish of the operator.''

TOWING OF LIFE-BOATS.

Reproduced from instructions published by the Royal National Life-Boat Institution of Great Britain.

On no account must any life-boat be towed, either by a steamer or sailing vessel, without her crew being in her, or at least a sufficient number of men to manage her in the event of her breaking adrift, or having to cast off from the towing vessel.

A life-boat may be towed with either one or two tow-ropes. If the former be adopted, it is recommended to tow with a long scope, from forty to sixty fathoms, the tow-rope being rove through a fair-leader or lizard at the stem head, and screwed to a bollard shipped in the trunk or tabernacle of the foremast.

If towed with two ropes, one from each quarter of the towing steamer, they should not be taken to the stem of the boat, but be made fast, one to each bow, for which purpose some life-boats are fitted with a bollard on each bow. In either case the crew should be seated well aft in the boat to weigh her by the stern, excepting one man forward with

6

a small hatchet by him, ready to cut the tow-rope in a moment if it should become necessary.

A life-boat will always be found to tow better against a heavy head sea than away from one, as there will be a more steady and regular strain on her, and she will tow less wildly and therefore with less violent jerks and strains on the tow-rope.

Great advantage is found when towing a life-boat before a heavy sea by towing a drogue astern of the boat to prevent her running ahead in front of a sea (at risk of damage against the towing vessel) and to keep up a more equable strain on the tow-rope.

INSTRUCTIONS FOR SAVING DROWNING PERSONS BY SWIMMING TO THEIR RELIEF.

1. When you approach a person drowning in the water, assure him, with a loud and firm voice, that he is safe.

2. Before jumping in to save him divest yourself as far and as quickly as possible of all clothes ; tear them off if necessary, but if there is not time, loose at all events the foot of your drawers if they are tied, as, if you do not do so, they will fill with water and drag you.

3. On swimming to a person in the sea, if he is struggling do not seize him then, but keep off for a few seconds till he gets quiet, for it is sheer madness to take hold of a man when he is struggling in the water, and if you do you run a great risk.

4. Then get close to him and take fast hold of the hair of his head, turn him as quickly as possible onto his back, give him a sudden pull, and this will cause him to float, then throw yourself on your back also and swim for the shore, both hands having hold of his hair, you on your back and he

also on his, and of course his back to your stomach. In this way you will get sooner and safer ashore than by any other means, and you can easily thus swim with two or three persons ; the writer has even, as an experiment, done it with four, and gone with them forty or fifty yards in the sea. One great advantage of this method is that it enables you to keep your head up, and also to hold the person's head up you are trying to save. It is of primary importance that you take fast hold of the hair'and throw both the person and yourself on your backs. After many experiments, it is usually found preferable to all other methods. You can in this manner float nearly as long as you please, or until a boat or other help can be obtained.

5. It is believed there is no such thing as a death-*grasp*, at least it is very unusual to witness it. As soon as a drowning man begins to get feeble and to lose his recollection, he gradually slackens his hold until he quits it altogether. No apprehension need, therefore, be felt on that head when attempting to rescue a drowning person.

6. After a person has sunk to the bottom, if the water be smooth, the exact position where the body lies may be known by the air-bubbles, which will occasionally rise to the surface, allowance being of course made for the motion of the water, if in a tide-way or stream, which will have carried the bubbles out of a perpendicular course in rising to the surface. A body may be often regained from the bottom before too late for recovery by diving for it in the direction indicated by these bubbles.

7. On rescuing a person by diving to the bottom, the hair of the head should be seized by one hand only, and the other used, in conjunction with the feet, in raising yourself and the drowning person to the surface.

8. If in the sea it may sometimes be a great error to try to get to land. If there be a strong out-setting tide, and you are swimming either by your-self, or having hold of a person who cannot swim, then get on your back and float till help comes. Many a man exhausts himself by stemming the billows for the shore on a back-going tide, and sinks in the effort, when, if he had floated, a boat or other aid might have been obtained.

9. These instructions apply alike to all circum-stances, whether as regards the roughest seâ or smooth water.

RULES FOR THE MANAGEMENT OF OPEN ROW BOATS IN A SURF—BEACHING THEM, ETC.

Reproduced from instructions published by the Royal National Life-Boat Institution of Great Britain.

I. *In rowing to seaward.*

As a general rule speed must be given to a boat rowing against a heavy surf. Indeed, under some circumstances, her safety will depend on the ut-most possible speed being attained on meeting a sea. For if the sea be really heavy, and the wind blowing a hard, on-shore gale, it can only be by the utmost exertions of the crew that any head-way can be made. The great danger, then, is that an approaching heavy sea may carry the boat away on its front, and turn it broadside on, or up end it, either effect being immediately fatal. A boat's only chance in such a case is to obtain such way as shall enable her to pass end on through the crest of the sea, and leave it as soon as possible behind her. Of course, if there be a rather heavy surf, but no wind, or the wind off shore and opposed to the surf, as is often the case, a boat might be propelled so rapidly through it that her bow would fall more suddenly and heavily after topping the sea than if her way had been checked ; and it may therefore only be when the sea is of such magnitude, and the boat of such a character, that there may be chance of the former carrying her back before it that full speed should be given her.

It may also happen that, by careful management under such circumstances, a boat may be made to avoid the sea, so that each wave may break ahead ·of her, which may be the only chance of safety in a small boat; but if the shore be flat, and the broken water extends to a great distance from it, this will often be impossible.

The following general rules for rowing to sea-·ward may, therefore, be relied on:

1. If sufficient command can be kept over a boat by the skill of those on board her, avoid or "dodge" the sea if possible, so as not to meet it at the moment of its breaking or curling over.

2. Against a head gale and heavy surf get all possible speed on a boat on the approach of every sea which cannot be avoided.

3. If more speed can be given to a boat than is sufficient to prevent her being carried back by a surf, her way may be checked on its approach, which will give her an easier passage over it.

II. *On running before a broken sea or surf to the shore.*

The one great danger when running before a broken sea is that of *broaching-to.* To that peculiar effect of the sea, so frequently destructive of human life, the utmost attention must be directed.

The cause of a boat's broaching-to when running before a broken sea or surf is that her own motion being in the same direction as that of the sea,

whether it be given by the force of oars or sails, or
by the force of the sea itself, she opposes no resistance to it, but is carried before it. Thus, if a boat
be running with her bow to the shore and her stern
to the sea, the first effect of the surf or roller, on
its overtaking her, is to throw up the stern, and
as a consequence to depress the bow; if she then
has sufficient inertia (which will be proportional
to weight) to allow the sea to pass her, she will in
succession pass through the descending, the horizontal, and the ascending positions, as the crest of·
the wave passes successively her stern, her mid-
ships, and her bow in the reverse order in which
the same positions occur to a boat propelled to
seaward against a surf. This may be defined as
the safe mode of running before a broken sea.

But if a boat, on being overtaken by a heavy
surf, has not sufficient inertia to allow it to pass
her, the first of the three positions above enumer-
ated alone occurs; her stern is raised high in the
air, and the wave carries the boat before it on its
front or unsafe side, sometimes with frightful veloc-
ity, the bow all the time deeply immersed in the
hollow of the sea; where the water, stationary or
comparatively so, offers a resistance, whilst the
crest of the sea, having the actual motion which
causes it to break, forces onward the stern or rear
end of the boat. A boat will, in this position sometimes, aided by careful oar-steerage, run a considerable distance until the wave has broken and expended itself. But it will often happen that if the
bow be low it will be driven under water, when, the
buoyancy being lost forward, whilst the sea presses
on the stern, the boat will be thrown (as it is termed)
end over end; or if the bow be high, or it be protected, as in most life-boats, by a bow air-chamber,
so that it does not become submerged, that the

resistance forward, acting on one bow, will slightly turn the boat's head, and the force of the surf being transferred to the opposite quarter, she will in a moment be turned round broadside by the sea, and be thrown by it on her beam-ends or altogether capsized. It is in this manner that most boats are upset in a surf, especially on flat coasts, and in this way many lives are annually lost among merchant seamen when attempting to land after being compelled to desert their vessels.

Hence it follows that the management of a boat, when landing through a heavy surf, must, as far as possible, be assimilated to that when proceeding to seaward against one, at least so far as to stop her progress shoreward at the moment of being overtaken by a heavy sea, and thus enabling it to pass her. There are different ways of effecting this object:

1. By turning a boat's head to the sea before entering the broken water, and then backing in stern foremost, pulling a few strokes ahead to meet each heavy sea, and then again backing astern. If a sea be really heavy and a boat small, this plan will be generally the safest, as a boat cannot be kept more under command when the full force of the oars can be used against a heavy surf than by backing them only.

2. If rowing to shore with the stern to seaward, by backing all the oars on the approach of a heavy sea, and rowing ahead again as soon as it has passed to the bow of the boat, thus rowing it on the back of the wave ; or, as is practiced in some life-boats, placing the after-oarsmen with their faces forward and making them row back at each sea on its approach.

3. If rowed in bow foremost, by towing astern a pig of ballast, or large stone, or a large basket, or

a canvas bag, termed a "drogue" or drag, made
for the purpose, the object of each being to hold
the boat's stern back, and to prevent her being
turned broadside to the sea or broaching-to.

Drogues are in common use by the boatmen on
the Norfolk coast ; they are conical-shaped bags of
about the same form and proportionate length and
breadth as a candle extinguisher, about two feet
wide at the mouth, and four and a half feet long.
They are towed with the mouth foremost by a stout
rope, a small line, being termed a tripping-line,
being fast to the apex or pointed end. When towed
with the mouth foremost they fill with water and
offer a considerable resistance, thereby holding back
the stern ; by letting go the stouter rope and retain-
ing the smaller line their position is reversed, when
they collapse, and can be readily hauled into the
boat.

Drogues are chiefly used in sailing-boats, when
they both serve to check a boat's way and to keep
her end on to the sea. They are, however, a great
source of safety in rowing-boats, and the rowing
life-boats of the National Life-Boat Institution are
now all provided with them.

A boat's sail bent to a yard and towed astern
loosed, the yard being attached to a line capable of
being veered, hauled or let go will act in some
measure as a drogue, and will tend much to break
the force of the sea immediately astern of the boat.

Heavy weights should be kept out of the extreme
ends of a boat ; but when rowing before a heavy
sea the best trim is deepest by the stern, which
prevents the stern being readily thrown on one
side by the sea.

A boat should be steered by an oar over the
stern, or on one quarter when running before a sea,
as the rudder will then at times be of no use. If

the rudder be shipped, it should be kept amidships on a sea breaking over the stern.

The following general rules may, therefore, be depended on when running before, or attempting to land through, a heavy surf or broken water :

1. As far as possible, avoid each sea by placing the boat where the sea will break ahead or astern of her.

2. If the sea be very heavy, or if the boat be very small, and especially if she have a square stern, bring her bow round to seaward and back her in, rowing ahead against each heavy surf that cannot be avoided sufficiently to allow it to pass the boat.

3. If it be considered safe to proceed to the shore bow foremost, back the oars against each sea on its approach, so as to stop the boat's way through the water as far as possible, and if there is a drogue, or any other instrument in the boat which may be used as one, tow it astern to aid in keeping the boat end on to sea, which is the chief object in view.

4. Bring the principal weights in the boat toward the end that is to seaward, but not to the extreme end.

5. If a boat worked by both sails and oars be running under sail for the land through a heavy sea, her crew should, under all circumstances, unless the beach be quite steep, take down her masts and sails before entering the broken water, and take her to land under oars alone, as above described. If she have sails only, her sails should be much reduced, a half-lowered foresail or other small head-sail being sufficient.

III. *Beaching or landing through a surf.*

The running before a surf or broken sea, and the

beaching or landing of a boat, are two distinct operations; the management of boats as above recommended has exclusive reference to running before a surf where the shore is so flat that the broken water extends to some distance from the beach. Thus, on a very steep beach, the first heavy fall of broken water will be on the beach itself, whilst on some very flat shores there will be broken water as far as the eye can reach, sometimes extending to even four or five miles from the land. The outermost line of broken water, on a flat shore, where the waves break in three or four fathoms water, is the heaviest, and, therefore, the most dangerous; and, when it has been passed through in safety, the danger lessens as the water shoals, until, on nearing the land, its force is spent and its power harmless.

As the character of the sea is quite different on steep and flat shores, so is the customary manage-ment of boats on landing different in the two situ-ations. On the flat shore, whether a boat be run or backed in, she is kept straight before or end on to the sea until she is fairly aground, when each surf takes her further in as it overtakes her, aided by the crew, who will then generally jump out to lighten her, and drag her in by her sides. As above stated, sail will in this case have been previously taken in if set, and the boat will have been rowed or backed in by oars alone.

On the other hand, on the *steep* beach it is the general practice, in a boat of any size, to retain speed right on to the beach, and in the act of landing, whether under oars or sail, to turn the boat's bow half round toward the direction from which the surf is running, so that she may be thrown on her broadside up the beach, where abundance of help is usually at hand to haul her as quickly as possible out of the reach of the sea. In such situations, we believe, it is nowhere the practice to back a boat in stern foremost under oars, but to row in under full speed, as above described.

IV. *Boarding a wreck or a vessel, under sail or at anchor, in a heavy sea.*

The circumstances under which life-boats or other boats have to board vessels, whether stranded or at anchor or under way, are so various that it would be impossible to draw up any general rule for guidance. Nearly everything must depend on the skill, judgment, and presence of mind of the coxswain or officer in charge of the boat, who will often have those qualities taxed to the utmost, as undoubtedly the operation of boading a vessel in a heavy sea or surf is frequently one of extreme danger.

It will be scarcely necessary to state that, whenever practicable, a vessel, whether stranded or afloat, should be boarded to leeward, as the principal dangers to be guarded against must be the violent collision of the boat against the vessel, or her swamping or upsetting by the rebound of the sea, or by its irregular direction in coming in contact with the vessel's side; and the greater violence of the sea on the windward side is much more likely to cause such accidents. The danger must, of course, also be still further increased when the vessel is aground and the sea breaking over her. The chief danger to be apprehended on boarding a stranded vessel on the lee side, if broadside to the sea, is the falling of the masts; or if they have been previously carried away, the damage or destruction of the boat amongst the floating spars and gear alongside. It may, therefore, under such circumstances, be often necessary to take a wrecked crew into a life-boat from the bow or stern ; otherwise a rowing-boat, proceeding from a lee shore to a wreck, by keeping under the vessel's lee, may use her as a breakwater, and thus go off in comparatively smooth water, or be at least shielded from the worst of the sea.   This is, accordingly, the usual practice in the rowing life-boats around the United Kingdom.   The larger sailing life-boats, chiefly on the Norfolk and Suffolk coasts, which go off to wrecks on outlying shoals, are, however, usually anchored to windward of stranded vessels, and then veered down to 100 or 150 fathoms of cable, until near enough to throw a line on board. The greatest care, under these circumstances, has, of course, to be taken to prevent actual contact between the boat and the ship, and the crew of the latter have sometimes to jump overboard and to be hauled to the boat by ropes.

In every case of boarding wreck or a vessel at sea, it is important that the lines by which a boat is made fast to the vessel should be of sufficient length to allow of her rising or falling freely with the sea ; and every rope should be kept in hand ready to cut or slip it in a moment if necessary. On wrecked persons or other passengers being taken into a boat in a sea way, they should be placed on the thwarts in equal numbers on either side, and be made to sit down.   All crowding or rushing headlong into the boat should be prevented as far as possible ; and the captain of a ship, if a wreck, should be called on to remain on board to preserve order until every other person had left her.

TREATMENT OF FROST-BITES, AS RECOMMENDED BY THE SURGEON-GENERAL MARINE HOSPITAL SERVICE.

1. Do not bring the patient to the fire, nor bathe the parts in warm water.

2. If snow be on the ground, or accessible, take a woollen cloth in the hand, place a handful of snow upon it, and gently rub the frozen part until the natural color is restored. In case snow is not at hand, bathe the part gently with a woollen cloth in the coldest *fresh* water obtainable—ice-water, if practicable.

3. In case the frost-bite is old, and the skin has turned black or begun to scale off, do not attempt to restore its vitality by friction, but apply carron oil on a little cotton ; after which wrap the part loosely in flannel.

4. In all cases, as soon as the vitality has been restored, apply the carron oil, prepared according to service formula. As it contains opium, do not administer morphia or other opiate.

5. In the case of a person apparently dead from exposure to cold, friction should be applied to the body and the lower extremities, and artificial respiration practiced as in case of the apparently drowned. As soon as the circulation appears to be restored, administer spirit and water at intervals of fifteen or twenty minutes until the flesh feels natural. Even if no signs of life appear, friction should be kept up for a long period, as instances are on record of recovery after several hours of suspended animation.

Carron Oil—(service formula):
Olive oil or linseed oil (raw);
Lime water, of each 12 parts;
Tincture of opium, 1 part.
Mix.

In the New York *Sportsman* of April, 1883, we find the following publication : ♦

TO PROFESSIONAL SWIMMERS.

WASHINGTON, D. C., *April* 24, 1883.

EDITOR SPORTSMAN : I am confident a professional swimming organization will be of great benefit to the profession as well as the public at large who are interested in the advancement of natatorial sport. I would like to see all the professional swimmers of this country in one organized body for protection and mutual benefit. A constitution and other laws could be made and adopted that would govern swimming matches and all questions arising from such contests. The association could, at a spring meeting, make out a programme of summer work, consisting of tournaments and all kinds of swimming contests that our leading watering resorts would gladly offer liberal purses to witness, and by this means we could bring before the public those who would accomplish feats of daring and endurance, with the guarantee that they were going to be paid for the same. The fact that we were acting under a national association would give prestige to anything we might do, and when some brave fellow at the risk of his life went to the assistance of his fellow-man and rescued him from a watery grave, we could give him honorable mention and otherwise reward the noble action, for it is too often the case that such deeds go unrewarded. A sinking fund could be created for the benefit of brothers in distress—perhaps a home established where *life savers* could find shelter when in need; and many persons there are in this country philanthropically inclined who would contribute to an institution of that kind.

Yours fraternally,   R. E. ODLUM.

The idea advocated is a most excellent one, and shows the necessity for such an organization. Risking one's life merely for the fun of it is not a lucrative business, and as the officers of the Army and Navy, subalterns and privates, are paid by the Government for performing brave acts, no reason exists why the swimmer who saves a human life should not have his reward   Fame is much to be coveted, but does not feed or clothe the hero unless the Government remembers him in appropriations.

The article shows that Professor Odlum was alive to the interests of his profession, and had there been any concert of action, a union such as he proposed would now be in existence to benefit professional swimmers in distress, thrown upon the rocks of financial misfortune, and a house established where life savers could find shelter from the storms of adversity.

THE UNITED STATES LIFE-SAVING SERVICE.

The United States is the only government in the world boasting a life-saving service.   The service in other countries being all voluntary societies supported by the donations of benevolent people, to this country belongs the eminent distinction of having organized an elaborate system of relief for seafarers wrecked upon its coast.   An appropriation of $5,000 made by Congress in 1847 was the commencement of the organization.   In August, 1848, Congress appropriated $10,000 for providing surf-boats and other appliances for rescuing life and property from shipwreck on the coast of New Jersey. In March, 1849, Congress made a further appropriation of $20,000 for life-saving purposes, and in 1850 Congress again appropriated $20,000 for life-saving purposes.   The life-saving service continued to grow in importance; the stations erected were found to be insufficient, and in the years 1853 and 1854 Congress appropriated $42,500, and fourteen new stations were erected on the New Jersey coast, and eleven on the coast of Long Island. Twenty-three life-boats were also placed at points upon Lake Michigan, and several others at various places on the Atlantic and lake coasts. Exclusive of the boats at the fifty-five stations on the New York and New Jersey coasts, there were in 1854 eighty-two life-boats at different localities elsewhere. Time and the weather soon destroyed these boats, or rendered them unfit for service. Heart-rending scenes of shipwreck and drowning occurred off our coast, and the life-boats had not met the public expectations. Public sentiment now excited Congress toward doing something in the matter. A bill for the increase and repair of the stations and the guardianship of the life-boats became a law in 1854. The frightful disaster on the New Jersey coast— the wreck of the Powhatan—involving the loss of three hundred lives, hastened the passage of the bill. Under this bill a superintendent at a compensation of $1,500 per annum was appointed for each of the two coasts, a keeper was assigned each station at a salary of $200, the stations and their equipments were made serviceable, and bonded custodians were secured for the life boats. Partial improvement in the service resulted, but the absence of drilled and disciplined crews, of regulations of any kind for the government of those concerned, and, above all, of energetic central administration of its affairs, were radical defects, and the record continued to be one of meager benefits, checkered by the saddest failures. In 1869 a bill was introduced in Congress providing for the employment of crews of surfmen at the stations, and

a substitute was adopted which secured the employ-
ment of these crews, though only at alternate stations.   This was a measure of signal benefit, chiefly
because it opened the door to the subsequent em-
ployment of crews at all the stations.

The year 1871 was the date of the organization
of the present life-saving system.   Order now began
to stream from chaos.   During the winter of 1870-'71
several fatal disasters, some of them occurring near
the stations, others at points where stations should
have been, and all referable to irresponsible em-
ployees, inadequate boats and apparatus or remote-
ness of life-saving appliances, roused the Treasury
Department to make proper representations to
Congress upon the subject, which, on April 20,
1871, appropriated $200,000, and authorized the
Secretary of the Treasury to employ crews of surfmen at such stations and for such periods as he
might deem necessary.   In the February previous
Mr. Sumner I. Kimball took charge of the Revenue
Marine Service, and the life-saving stations being
then under the charge of that bureau also became
the subject of his consideration.   Uniting with a
thorough knowledge of his position a zeal and industry in his work, his first step was to ascertain
their condition.   At his instance Capt. John Faunce
was detailed for this duty, and started on a tour of
inspection of the stations, Mr. Kimball accompany-
ing him a part of the way.   Captain Faunce's report was submitted in August, 1871, and all the
defects found were quickly remedied, and the life-
saving service was given a new impetus, and grew
in the favor of the people, and rendered invaluable
service in saving the cargoes and ships' crews from
watery graves.   Under the able administration of
Mr. Kimball the United States Life-Saving Service
has become a pride to the Government, and with

7

the reforms the new life-saving apparatus, boats,
&c., to be introduced, the dangers of the deep, the
dreaded breakers that come rushing in from the
sea will be looked upon as comparatively harmless.
Knowledge, bravery, and zeal accomplish much,
especially where the Government tenders the aid
of its powerful assistance. These traits are possessed by Superintendent Kimball. The record of
the past years show how much good has been accomplished by the life-saving service under its
present able management. The future can only
add more to the efficiency of the service and confirm
the wisdom of Congress in organizing the bureau

From the report of the service of the year 1884
we find a—

*General summary of disasters which have occurred within the scope
of life-saving operations from November 1, 1871, (date of introduction of present system,) to close of fiscal year ending June
30, 1884:*

Total number of disasters	2,547
Total value of vessels	$31,665,600
Total value of cargoes	$15,463,714
Total value of property involved	$47,129,314
Total value of property saved	$32,898,346
Total value of property lost	$14,230,968
Total number of persons involved	23,217
Total number of persons saved	22,771
Total number of lives lost	446
Total number of persons succored	4,261
Total number of days succor afforded	11,627

The United States Life-Saving Service is almost
perfect in all its working details. The keeper of
each station selects his own crew, who are, however, subject to the decision of the examining board.
He is an inspector of customs, having the care of
all stranded property, and authority for the pre-
vention of smuggling. He keeps the station and

equipments in order, commands the crew, steers
the boats to wrecks, and conducts all the operations.
They reside constantly with their crews during the
active season.

The scheme of the service places the long chain
of complete life-saving stations on the Atlantic
beaches within an average distance of each other.
The lack of fresh water on the beaches is one of
the hardships of station life.

The life-boat stations are usually twenty-four
feet high from base to peak, forty-two feet long by
twenty-two feet wide, exterior measurement, and
contain a loft above, and a room below, twelve feet
high, twenty feet wide, and forty feet long, for the
accommodation of the life-boat and its gear.

It is not my intention to enter into minute details of the general make-up of the life-saving service, but it may be interesting to note the cost to
the Government in maintaining the system.   The
Government receives no pecuniary recompense and
the grand object is to act the part of the Good
Samaritan to persons in distress.

A complete life-saving station fully equipped
costs about $5,000, a life-boat station about $4,500,
and a house of refuge about $3,000.

The reports of the life-saving service from the
organization of the service to the present time are
of peculiar interest, and form interesting, lively
reading.   The name of every ship or vessel in distress saved or aided by the life-saving service is
given, with a full and minute account of the circumstances.   Persons fond of such reading will be
well paid by a perusal.   The accounts are written
in a plain, sensible manner, and are almost, if not
fully, equal to Robinson Crusoe, and have truth
also for a foundation, which Robinson Crusoe has
not.

The life of the keepers, and the duty devolving upon the brave crews of surfmen require extraordinary courage, coolness, and discretion. One unacquainted with the sea can have but little idea of its fury during a storm, when the angry billows chase each other and waste their anger on the shores ; when the waves run mountain high ; when a ship becomes unmanageable, and is at the sport of the wind ; when the vessel runs aground and the waves break over the decks ; when the stormy petrel—the bird of bad omen—screams with delight above the blast, and seems delighted with the dreadful surroundings—brave must be the surfmen's hearts, strangers to fear, who risk their life in an attempt to save a wreck in such an hour.

Congress on the 20th of June, 1874, passed an act granting gold medals to those who distinguished themselves by special acts of daring on these dangerous adventures. Two *only* are given out annually, and the rivalry among the brave men to secure a medal can be better imagined than described.

Should a brave surfman lose his life in the perilous undertaking of rescuing others, it becomes the duty of the Government to provide handsomely for those he may leave behind who were dependent on his bounty. A medal is a badge of honor, but the comforts and necessaries of life are sternly demanded. Congress should be generously inclined to the brave men who do honor to the life-saving service by their gallant deeds.

The laws made for the government of the life-saving service are very plain, and are administered with the strictness of military regulations. The rules are laid down with precision. Each man in the service has his duty to perform, and has to perform it. It is necessary in a service like this to have a surgeon to care for the sick and wounded serfmen, and to be ready to afford means for the resuscitation of individuals taken from the water. I had the fortune to rescue the body of G. Fred Ruff from the waves, at Fortress Monroe, and we did everything in our power to resuscitate him, but in vain. In a few days after the sad affair I received the following letter:

U. S. MARINE HOSPITAL SERVICE,
BALTIMORE, *August* 8, 1882.

Mr. R. E. ODLUM,
Hygeia Hotel, Old Point Comfort, Va.

MY DEAR SIR: I send you the printed instructions concerning resuscitation as practiced in the lifesaving service. The method described is a good one. There are two other methods.

"The *Marshall Hall method* consists in laying the patient on his face on the floor or on a table and then turning him on his back. By this means the weight of the body compresses the chest while it expands again by the natural elasticity of the ribs."

"The *Sylvester method* is easier of application, and has now been generally adopted by the Royal Humane Society. The patient should be laid on his back, and then both his arms should be raised above his head, held there for a second or two and brought down again on the sides of the chest with some degree of pressure. After the lapse of two seconds the process should be repeated."

The principle in all methods is the same, viz., to expand the thoracic cavity, in other words, the chest, and then to contract it, in imitation of the natural movements of inspiration and expiration.

"Whatever plan is adopted, the steps of the

process should be repeated about fifteen times per minute, steadily and with regularity.''

It was the Sylvester method practically which I adopted in the case of Mr. Ruff, and I chose it because I was familiar with it and had used it successfully twice before.

When I found that all the helpers were exhausted I began the Marshall Hall method as being easier and requiring but one person, and, you will remember, was endeavoring to get you to carry it out when the other physician announced, ''Oh, he's gone,'' which encouraging sentiment was so strongly echoed by the by-standers as to prevent any one else lending a helping hand.

I do not believe the result could have been changed, but if I could have had my own way I should have kept on working at least an hour and a half longer. I only mention this to warn you from desisting too soon if you should have another case, and *not* be guided by this experience as to the length of time you keep up artificial respiration. Note that the printed instructions say ''one to four hours.''

I would recommend that you get some good, stout fellow and practice artificial respiration on him by these different methods in succession.

I think you deserve great credit for your perseverance and ability in getting Mr. Ruff out of the water, and as your calling makes it probable that you may see more cases, and gives you so much authority at the time, I have thought you would appreciate these lines on artificial respiration.

Hoping you will take them in good part,

I am, very respectfully,

WALTER WYMAN,
Surgeon U. S. M. H. S.

RESUSCITATION.

When a man has fallen overboard and is apparently drowned, all means possible should be taken to restore him to life. The following are the directions of the United States Life-Saving Service, which have been found to be useful in such cases:

RULE I. *Arouse the patient.*—Unless in danger of freezing, do not move the patient, but instantly expose the face to a current of fresh air, wipe dry the mouth and nostrils, rip the clothing, so as to expose the chest and waist, and give two or three quick, smarting slaps on the stomach and chest with the open hand. If the patient does not revive, then proceed thus:

RULE II. *To draw off water, &c., from the stomach and chest.*—If the jaws are clinched separate them, and keep the mouth open by placing between the teeth a cork or small bit of wood ; turn the patient on the face, a large bundle of tightly-rolled clothing being placed beneath the stomach, and press heavily over it for half a minute, or so long as fluids flow freely from the mouth.

RULE III. *To produce breathing.*—Clear the mouth and throat of mucus, by introducing into the throat the corner of a handkerchief wrapped closely around the forefinger ; turn the patient on the back, the roll of clothing being so placed beneath it as to raise the pit of the stomach above the level of any other part of the body. If there be another person present let him, with a piece of dry cloth, hold the tip of the tongue out of one corner of the mouth (this prevents the tongue from falling back and choking the entrance to the windpipe), and with the other hand grasp both wrists and keep the arms forcibly stretched back above the head, thereby increasing the prominence of the ribs, which tends to enlarge the chest. The two last-named positions are not, however, essential to success. Kneel beside or astride the patient's hips, and with the balls of the thumbs resting on either side of the pit of the stomach, let the fingers fall into the grooves between the short ribs, so as to afford the best grasp of the waist. Now, using your knees as a pivot, throw all your weight forward on your hands, and at the same time squeeze the waist between them, as if you wished to force everything in the chest upward out of the mouth ; deepen the pressure while you can count slowly one, two, three ; then suddenly let go with a final push, which springs you back to your first kneeling position. Remain erect on your knees while you can count one, two, three ; then repeat the same motions as before at a rate gradually increased from four or five to fifteen times in a minute, and continue thus this bellows movement with the same regularity that is observable in the natural motions of breathing which you are imitating. If the natural breathing be not restored, after a trial of the bellows movement for the space of three or four minutes, then, without interrupting the artificial respiration, turn the patient a second time on the stomach, as directed in Rule II, rolling the body in the opposite direction from that in which it was first turned, for the purpose of freeing the air-passages from any remaining water. Continue the artificial respiration with pressure and energy, using the bare hands, dry flannels, or handkerchiefs, and continuing the friction under the blankets or over the dry clothing. The warmth of the body can also be promoted by the application of hot flannels to the stomach and arm-pits, bottles or bladders of hot water, heated bricks, &c., to the limbs and soles of the feet.

RULE IV. AFTER-TREATMENT. — *Externally:* As soon as breathing is established let the patient be stripped of all wet clothing, wrapped in blankets only, put to bed comfortably warm, but with a free circulation of fresh air, and left to perfect rest. *Internally:* Give a little brandy and hot water, or other stimulant at hand, every ten or fifteen minutes for the first hour, and as often thereafter as may seem expedient. *Later manifestations:* After reaction is fully established there is great danger of congestion of the lungs, and if perfect rest is not maintained for at least forty-eight hours, it sometimes occurs that the patient is seized with great difficulty of breathing, and death is liable to follow unless immediate relief is afforded. In such cases apply a large mustard-plaster over the breast. If the patient gasps for breath before the mustard takes effect, assist the breathing by carefully repeating the artificial respiration.

In an old volume of the year 1839 I find mention made of a celebrated English swimmer, who was one of a class called beachmen on the shores of England. In my leisure hours I derive much pleasure in searching up the names of men celebrated in any profession. History mentions the great generals and admirals of all ages, but peace hath her victories no less renowned than war, and many a noble fellow, following an humble profession, had as brave a heart, and oftentimes a better, kinder feeling in his bosom for his fellow man than the greatest warrior of ancient or modern times. The hero who saves a life is greater than the general who slaughters a thousand or ransacks a city.

In this old volume I find a long account of a brave
man, whose daring was an honor to his parents
and friends.   I propose to give an account of—

BROCK, THE SWIMMER.

Among the sons of labor there are none more
deserving of their hard earnings than that class of
persons denominated beachmen.   To those unacquainted with maritime affairs it may be as well to
observe that these men are bred to the sea from
their earliest infancy, are employed in the summer
months very frequently as regular sailors or fisher-
men, and during the autumn, winter and spring,
when gales are most frequent on our coast, in going off in boats to vessels in distress in all weathers
to the imminent risk of their lives ; fishing up
lost anchors and cables and looking out for waifs
which the winds and waves may cast in their way.
In our seaports these persons are usually divided
into companies, between whom the greatest rivalry
exists in regard to the beauty and swiftness of their
boats, and their dexterity in managing them. This
too often leads to feats of the greatest daring, which
the widow and the orphan have long to deplore.
To one of these companies, known by the name of
"Layton's," whose rendezvous and "look-out"
is close to Yarmouth Jetty, Brock belongs, and in
pursuit of his calling the following event is recorded :
About 1 p. m. on the 6th of October, 1835, a
vessel was observed at sea from this station with a
signal flying for a pilot, bearing east, distant about
twelve miles.   In a space of time incredible for
those who have not witnessed the launching of a
large boat on a like occasion, the yawl "Increase,"
eighteen tons burden, belonging to Layton's gang,

with ten men and a London Branch pilot was under way steering for the object of their enterprise. "I was as near as possible being left ashore," said Brock to me, "for at the time the boat was getting down to the breakers I was looking at Manby's apparatus for saving the lives of persons on a wreck then practicing, and but for the 'singing-out' of my messmates, which caught my ear, should have been too late, but I reached in time to jump in with wet feet."

About 4 o'clock they came up with the vessel, which proved to be a Spanish brig, Paquette de Bilboa, laden with a general cargo and bound from Hamburg to Cadiz, leaky and both pumps at work. After a great deal of chaffering and haggling in regard to the amount of salvage and some little altercation with part of the boat's crew as to which of them should stay with the vessel, T. Layton, (a Gatt pilot,) J. Woolsey and George Darling, boatmen, were finally chosen to assist in pumping and piloting her into Yarmouth harbor; the remainder of the crew of the yawl were then sent away. The brig at this time was about five miles to the eastward of the Newarp floating light off Winterton, on the Norfolk coast, the weather looking squally. On passing the light in their homeward course a signal was made for them to go alongside, and they were requested to take on shore a sick man, and the poor fellow being comfortably placed upon some jackets and spare coats, they again shoved off and set all sail (three lugs ;) they had a fresh breeze from the W. S. W. And now again my readers shall have Brock's own words:

"There was little better than a pint of liquor in the boat, which the Spaniard had given us, and the bottle had passed once around, each man taking a mouthful, and about half of it was thus consumed.

Most of us had got a bit of bread or biscuit in his
hand, making a sort of light meal, and into the
bargain I had hold of the main sheet. We had
passed the buoy of the Newarp a few minutes, and
the light was about two miles astern; we had talked
of our job, *i. e.*, our earnings, and had just calculated that by 10 o'clock we should be at Yarmouth."

> "Alas! nor wife nor children more shall they behold,
>   Nor friends, nor sacred home."

Without the slightest notice of its approach a
terrific squall from the northward took the yawl's
sails flat aback, and the ballast, which they had
trimmed to windward, being thus suddenly changed
to leeward, she was upset in an instant. Her crew
and passengers were nine in number.

> "Then rose from sea to sky the wild farewell."

But perhaps Brock's words on this occasion will
excite more interest than Byron's: "'Twas terrible to listen to the cries of the poor fellows, some
of whom could swim, and others who could not.
Mixed with the hissing of the water and the howl-
ings of the storm, I heard shrieks for mercy, and
some that had no meaning but what arose from
fear. I struck out to get clear of the crowd, and
in a few minutes there was no noise, for most of
the men had sunk, and, on turning around, I saw
the boat was still kept from going down by the
wind having got under the sails. I then swam
back to her, and assisted an old man to get hold of
one of her spars. The boat's side was about three
feet under water, and for a few minutes I stood
upon her, but I found she was gradually settling
down, and when up to my chest I again left her
and swam away, and now for the first time began

to think of my own awful condition. My companions were all drowned, at least I supposed so. How long it was up to this period from the boat's capsizing I cannot exactly say; in such cases, sir, there is no time, but now I reflected that it was half past 6 p. m. just before the accident occurred; that the nearest land at the time was *six miles distant;* that it was dead low water, and the flood tide *setting off the shore,* making to the southward, therefore should I ever reach the land it would take me at least fifteen miles up against the flood before the ebb would assist me."

At this moment a rush horse collar, covered with old netting, which had been used as one of the boat's fenders, floated closer to him, which he laid hold of, and getting his knife out he stripped it of the net-work, and, by putting his left arm through it, was supported till he had cut the waistband of his petticoat trousers, which then fell off; his striped frock, waistcoat and neckcloth were also similarly got rid of, but he dared not try to free himself of his oiled trousers, drawers or shirt, fearing that his legs might become entangled in the attempt; he therefore returned his knife into the pocket of his trousers, and put the collar over his head, which, although it assisted in keeping him above water, retarded his swimming, and after a few moments thinking what was best to be done, he determined to abandon it. He now, to his great surprise, perceived one of his messmates swimming ahead of him, but he did not hail him. The roaring of the hurricane was past; the cries of drowning men were no longer heard, and the moonbeams were casting their silvery light over the smooth surface of the deep, calm and silent as the grave over which he floated, and into which he saw the last of his companions descend without a struggle

or a cry as he approached within twenty yards of
him.   Yes, he beheld the last of his brave crew die
beside him, and now he was alone in the cold,
silent loneliness of night, more awful than the
strife of the elements which had preceded.   Perhaps at this time something might warn him that
he too would soon be mingled with the dead—

> "With not one friend to animate and tell
> To others' ears that death became him well."

But if such thoughts did intrude, they were but
for a moment; and again his mental energies,
joined with his lion heart and bodily prowess, cast
away all fear, and he reckoned the remotest possible chances of deliverance, applying the means—

> "Courage and Hope both teaching him the practice."

Up to this time Winterton light had served,
instead of a land-mark, to direct his course, but the
tide had now carried him out of sight of it, and in
its stead "a bright star stood over where his hopes
of safety rested."   With his eyes steadfastly fixed
upon it he continued swimming on, calculating the
time when the tide would turn.   But his trials
were not yet past.   As if to prove the power of
human fortitude, the sky became suddenly over-
clouded, and "darkness was upon the face of the
deep."   He no longer knew his course, and he con-
confessed that for a moment he was afraid; yet he
felt that "fear is but the betraying of the succors
which reason offereth," and that which roused *him*
to further exertion would have sealed the fate of
almost any other human being—a sudden short
cracking peal of thunder burst in stunning loud-
ness just over his head, and the forked and flashing
lightning at brief intervals threw its vivid fires

around him. This, too, in its turn, passed away
and left the wave once more calm and unruffled ;
the moon (nearly full) again threw a more brilliant
light upon the bosom of the sea, which the storm
had gone over without waking from its slumbers.
His next effort was to free himself from his heavy
laced boots, which greatly encumbered him, and in
which he succeeded by the aid of his knife.   He
now saw Lowestoft high lighthouse, and could
occasionally discern the tops of the cliffs beyond
Gorlestone, on the Suffolk coast.   The swell of the
sea drove him over the Cross sand ridge, and he
then got sight of a buoy, which, although it told .
him his exact position, as he says, " took him rather
aback," as he had hoped he was nearer the shore.
It proved to be the chequered buoy of St. Nicholas
Gatt, off Yarmouth, and *opposite his own door*, but
distant from the land *four miles*.   And now again
he held council with himself, and the energies of
his mind seem almost superhuman ; he had been
five hours in the water, and there was something
to hold on by ; he could have even got upon the
buoy, and some vessel *might come near* to pick him
up, and the question was, could he yet hold out
four miles ?.   " But," as he says, " I knew the night
air would soon finish me, and had I stayed but a
few minutes upon it, and then *altered* my mind,
how did I know that my limbs would again resume
their office ?"   He found the tide (to use a sea
term) was broke ; it did not run so strong, so he
abandoned the buoy and steered for the land, toward which, with the wind from the eastward, he
found he was now fast approaching.   The last trial
of his fortitude was now at hand, for which he was
totally unprepared, and which he considers (sailors
being not a little superstitious) the most difficult of
any he had to combat.   Soon after he left the buoy

he heard just above his head a whizzing sound, which his imagination conjured into the prelude to the "rushing of a mighty wind," and close to his ear there followed a smart splash in the water, and a sudden shriek that went through him, such as is heard—

"When the lone sea bird wakes its wildest cry."

The fact was, a large gray gull, mistaking him for a corpse, had made a dash at him, and its loud discordant scream in a moment had brought a countless number of these formidable birds together, all prepared to contest for and share the spoil.

These large and powerful foes he had now to scare from their intended prey, and, by shouting and splashing with his hands and feet, in a few minutes they vanished from sight and hearing.

He now caught sight of a vessel at anchor, but a great way off, and to get within hail of her he must swim over Corton sands, (the grave of thousands,) the breakers at this time showing their angry white crests. As he approached, the wind suddenly changed, the consequence of which was that the swell of the sea met him. And now again for his own description:

"I got a great deal of water down my throat, which greatly weakened me, and I felt certain that, should this continue, it would soon be all over, and I prayed that the wind might change, or that God would take away my senses before I felt what it was to drown. In less time than I am telling you, I had driven over the sand into smooth water; *the wind and swell came again from the eastward*, and my strength returned to me as fresh as in the beginning."

He now felt assured that he could reach the

shore, but he considered it would be better to get within hail of the brig, some distance to the southward of him, and the most difficult task of the two, as the ebb-tide was now running, which, although it carried him toward the land, set to the northward, and to gain the object of his choice would require much greater exertion. But here comes Brock again :

"If I gained the shore could I get out of the surf, which at that time was heavy on the beach ? and supposing I succeeded in this point, should I be able to walk, climb the cliffs and get to a house? if not, there was little chance of life remaining long in me ; but if I could make myself heard on board the brig, then I should secure immediate assistance. I got within two hundred yards of her, the nearest possible approach, and, summoning all my strength, I sung out as well as if I had been on shore."

He was answered from the deck, a boat was instantly lowered, and at half past 1 a. m., having swam seven hours in an October night, he was safe on board the brig Betsy of Sunderland, coal laden, at anchor in Corton Roads, fourteen miles from the spot where the boat was capsized. The captain's name was Christian.

Once safe on board, "Nature cried enough," he fainted, and continued insensible for some time. All that humanity could suggest was done for him by Christian and his crew ; they had no spirits on board, but they had bottled ale, which they made warm, and by placing Brock before a good fire, rubbing him dry, and putting him in hot blankets, he was at length with great difficulty enabled to get a little of the ale down his throat, but it caused excruciating pain, as his throat was in a state of high inflammation from breathing (as a swimmer does) so long the saline particles of sea and air, and it was now swollen very much, and, as he says, he feared he should be suffocated. He, however, after a little time fell into a sleep, which refreshed and strengthened him, but he awoke to intense bodily suffering. Round his neck and chest he was perfectly flayed ; the soles of his feet, his hands, and his hamstrings were also equally excoriated. In this state at about 9 a. m., the brig getting under weigh with the tide, he was put on shore at Lowestoft, in Suffolk, and immediately dispatched a messenger to Yarmouth with the sad tidings of the fate of the yawl and the rest of her crew.

Being now safely housed under the roof of a relative, with good nursing and medical assistance, in five days from the time of the accident, with a firm step he walked back to Yarmouth to confirm the wonderful rumors circulated respecting him, and to receive the congratulations of his friends and kindred.

In contemplating the feat of this extraordinary man it must appear to every one that his bodily prowess, gigantic as it is, appears as dust in the balance compared with the powers of his mind. To think and to judge rightly under some of the most appalling circumstances that ever surrounded mortal man—to reject the delusive for the more arduous ; to resolve and to execute—form such a combination of the best and rarest attributes of our nature, that where are we to look for them in the same man?

REMINISCENCES OF SAM PATCH.

Sam Patch, the father of the jumping business, rivals Charley Ross as a household character. He made his first leap at Niagara Falls October 6,

1829, from a rock seventy feet above the water. That didn't hurt him much, and on the 17th of the same month he made a second leap from a scaffold at the foot of the Biddle staircase. At the foot of the stairs Sam Patch rigged up a ladder one hundred feet high, climbed to the top, and then jumped down into the water, to show, as he said, that some things could be done as well as others. Then he went to the Genesee Falls and made a leap on November 6, 1829, less than a week before he made the jump which killed him.

Sam Patch's leap at Passaic Falls was September 30, 1827. He jumped from the foot of the whitened pine on the edge of the precipice overhanging the basin. He bounded off with a great leap and struck the water eighty or ninety feet below, feet first. He swam ashore. Many Paterson boys afterward safely followed Patch's example in making the leap.

This account of Sam Patch's last leap is taken from Mr. Henry B. Stanton's " Recollections:"

Sam Patch, the famous jumper and diver, came to Rochester in the fall, we will say, of 1828, and proposed to leap from the falls in the heart of the village. On the day fixed Sam appeared. The banks of the river as far as the eye could reach were lined with spectators. He was dressed in a suit of white, and I will state for the benefit of other fools of the same class that before he leaped he placed his hands firmly on his loins, then sprang from the shelving rock, and went down straight as an arrow. He came up feet foremost, and swam ashore amid the shouts of thousands. A few days later he proposed to leap again. He erected a scaffold twenty-five feet high on the brink of the falls, making the descent one hundred and twenty-five feet. On the day named another immense

throng assembled. Mr. Weed and I happened to
meet at the foot of the scaffold. Patch came dressed
as before, and apparently a little under the influence of liquor. As he ascended the scaffold Mr.
Weed left, but I remained. As Patch went down
his arms were all in a whirl, and he struck the
water with a stunning splash. The crowd waited
for hours. He did not rise. The next spring the
mangled remains of the poor wretch were found
at the foot of the falls at Carthage, four miles below.

When Sam made his last leap he was so drunk
that he could barely stand. But he could make a
speech, and did. It was :

" Napoleon was a great man and a great general.
He conquered armies and he conquered nations,
but he couldn't jump the Genesee Falls. Welling-
ton was a great man and a great soldier. He conquered Napoleon, but he couldn't jump the Genesee
Falls. That was left for me to do, and I can do it
and will."

A SWIM FOR LIFE IN THE ATLANTIC.

On the 16th of May, 1884, one of the large New
York packet ships was dashing along gallantly on
her course toward Europe with all sail set and a fine
breeze. The bright sun and cloudless sky over-
head, together with the quietness which reigned
over the ship's deck, (it being dinner hour all the
passengers were below,) made it a scene which the
lover of nature would admire ; and a feeling of
safety and confidence in the good ship, as she
scudded away before the wind, impressed itself on
the mind of the beholder, when, alas ! for the uncertainty of human hopes, one of the sailors, who
was at work on the extreme end of the main-yard, in
a lurch of the ship, lost his hold, and was precipi-

tated from the dizzy height into the sea. A wild
shriek, and a cry of "man overboard!" ran like
an electric shock fore and aft the ship. "Hard
up the helm ; let go the main tack ; haul up the
mainsail," sung out our first officer, a brave and
excellent seaman, at the same time running to the
stern of the ship with the life-buoy in his hand, he
cast it with all his might in the direction of the
poor sailor, who was already far astern, but without effect, for the spray blinded the struggling
man's sight and he never saw it. Others were
now loosening the ropes connecting the quarter-
boat to its iron supporters. The sailors, obstructed
in their actions by the pressure of the passengers,
who crowded around with terror depicted on their
faces, clambered into the boat before the ropes
were free, and, terrible to relate, they gave
way, and the boat, with five men in it, fell into
the sea; but quick as thought the hardy fellows
recovered themselves, got into the boat again as
she floated alongside the mighty hull of the ship,
and with a cheer they started off to save their fellow
man. No sooner had they started when their boat
began to fill with water, and they discovered when
nearly fifty yards off that in the fall of the boat her
side got stove, and made a wide breach for the sea
to flow in. This fresh misfortune all on the poop
of the ship perceived, and the fearful probability
forced itself on us that all would perish, when, with
the speaking-trumpet to his mouth, our officer
shouted, "Give way, my lads; 'tis a life-boat, she
can't sink." "Hurrah! Hurrah!" cried the gallant
tars, and away they went in the direction pointed
out by one of the officers in the mizzen rigging,
who, with a telescope, from the first moment had
kept his eye steadily fixed on the unfortunate man,
who, appearing and disappearing with every roll

of the billows, was battling with the crested Atlantic waves for his life. By this time the ship was hove to, and though every possible exertion was used, it was nearly fifteen minutes before the boat was under full way on her mission of rescue, and the sailor, fully four miles away, was now a mere speck on the vast ocean, visible only to those who had an elevated position on the ship's poop. Owing to the boat being so much nearer the surface of the sea, those in her could not discern their object, and had to be guided for a long time by the direction pointed out by the officers on board the ship. With straining eyes and ears every soul on board watched the quick dash of the gallant life-boat as she foamed through the surges, although half full of water, and with fluttering hearts and anxious hopes we observed through the telescope that the poor sailor still held up, and now and again we heard, or fancied we heard, a faint "halloo" borne over the deep.

At last, after a space of twenty minutes of the most intense suspense, the united joyous cheer of the boat's crew assured us that he was rescued. With that cheer the pent-up feelings of the passengers broke loose, and the ladies cried aloud, so agitated had they been during that fearful struggle of the poor sailor for his life.

Soon afterward the poor fellow was got on board utterly exhausted. We wrapped him up warmly, gave him a cordial draught, and after a sleep of an hour, during which he was continually making convulsive efforts with his hands and feet, he was sufficiently recovered to tell us, but with difficulty, for his nervous system had evidently received a severe shock, that after his fall, and when he rose to the surface, his first act was to throw off his great sea boots, the weight of which alone was suf-

ficient to sink him ; then, not being a good swimmer, he merely kept himself afloat without trying
to make any progress in the water, for as the ship
was going at the rate of ten knots an hour, she
seemed actually to fly away from him, until he
saw her sails put aback, then he could discern us
all on the poop, but the boat being lowered on the
opposite side, where he could not see it, he feared
we could not see *him*, and thought we did not lower
a boat on that account.   His feelings were dreadful; he gave himself up as lost, and every action of
.his life came before him as in a mirror.   He must
have swooned before the boat got to him, for his
first feeling of consciousness was when he was
caught by the boatswain and lifted into the boat,
and he thanked the Lord for his providential deliv- ·
erance.   His rescuers were made the lions of the
day, and the whole evening was taken up with
wonderful stories of " accidents by flood and field."

HOW DONALDSON DID IT.

Mr. R. Donaldson, a Scotchman, who is in the sad-
dlery business at No. 60 Warren street, made two
successful jumps from High Bridge on August 12
and 18, 1880.   He was brought up in Sunderland,
England, and began early by jumping from dock
walls and the sides of vessels.   Then he went
higher, to bowsprits and mainyards ; then to the
Sunderland Bridge, and finally to the royal yard
of the ship Charity, of Liverpool, a height of one
hundred and forty feet.   He was alone when he
first jumped at High Bridge, and wore a suit of
tights.   The police thought he was a suicide and
ran to catch him, but he jumped before they could
reach him.   He was not molested on his second
trial, and a large crowd watched him.   His fall

took 4½ seconds. The height was one hundred and twenty-four feet, and the water ten feet deep. After striking he skimmed under the water for a distance of fourteen feet. A brisk wind had slightly disturbed his equilibrium on the second trial, and he struck partly on his hip, but was not injured.

In describing his actions and sensations, Mr. Donaldson said last evening :

"I placed my feet closely together and spread my hands palms upward before my face. I then doubled up and sprang gently forward just far enough to clear the bridge. I held my head forward and shut my eyes. I paid no attention to my breathing ; that never occasions any trouble, and all this talk about losing breath when falling is nonsense. As I went down I straightened out naturally, and the wind rushed up past me at a terrible rate. The shock on my arms and chin was as if I had been struck with a board."

I have secured the following particulars of the death of Captain Webb. He was my devoted friend, and his loss will be severely felt by me. It is sad to think that after encountering so many perils he should have found a watery grave, and perished as he did. He died as a brave man, and his memory will always be dear to me.

CAPTAIN WEBB'S LAST SWIM.

Captain Webb and his business agent, Frederick Kyle, of Boston, left this city shortly before 12 o'clock yesterday and took the noon train on the New York Central to the Falls. They were driven in the Clifton House omnibus to that hotel, on the Canada side. Here they passed the time very quietly, Webb affably conversing with whoever chose to address him. His manner was genial and

exceedingly gentlemanly. He responded freely to
all questions that were asked him, and his pleasant,
hearty manner instantly won the favor and good
will of all who approached him.

During a long conversation with a representative
of the *Courier* he conversed in a highly intelligent
manner on a variety of subjects. He related some
of his experiences in the merchant navy of Great
Britain, and referred in a modest manner to some
of his aquatic achievements. He did not appear
particularly concerned about the hazardous feat he
was about to undertake, and when any doubt was
suggested in regard to his making the attempt, he
assured the doubter in firm but quiet terms of his
absolute intention to try to do what he had said
he would. He said more than once that he did not
anticipate any trouble, but though he spoke confidently, there was no trace of braggadocio in his
manner. He chatted pleasantly until the dinner
hour at the hotel. Strange to say he declined par-
taking of the meal, saying that he preferred not to
eat, adding, in a hearty English way, " I can keep
my wind better, you know, on an empty stomach."
He smoked a cigar, and sat quietly on the veranda
of the Clifton House.

So the time passed until 4 o'clock, when Mr.
Kyle took him aside and said a few words to him.
He then left the piazza, walked a short distance
along the road, and turned off down the steep path-
way leading down to McCloy's ferryboat house,
which is several hundred yards above the new suspension bridge, on the Canada shore. McCloy and
Webb had a brief conversation. The latter also
spoke to Mrs. McCloy, who asked him whether he
would see his wife and children again. He replied
confidently, " I hope to." He spoke about his
baby, seven months old, his wife and other child,

and said that he expected to meet them in a few
days at Nantasket. McCloy got the boat, a small
scow painted bottle-green, in readiness and two
pairs of oars, and Webb stepped steadily and cheerfully into it. "Time is up," he remarked to Mc-
Cloy, as the latter rowed the boat carefully out
through the rocks into the stream.

Arrived in the center of the stream, McCloy
slowly hauled under the new suspension bridge, on
which only a few persons were congregated to see the
daring man-fish start on his venturesome journey.
In utter silence, save the hoarse murmur of the
cataract, the scow made its way. Gradually the
current grew stronger, and the speed became cor-
respondingly greater. Very few words passed between the two men, save that the ferryman asked
Webb whether he had swam often before, to which
he replied: "Many times." "Have you ever seen
the rapids?" asked McCloy. Webb answered:
"I've had a glimpse of them." In answer to
McCloy's questions he said he had made $25,000
by swimming the English channel, and he had
$15,000 left. McCloy states that he advised him
to go ashore and spend it, and not risk his life in
the rapids.   .

A few moments later McCloy told the hardy
swimmer that he had brought him as far as he
could with safety to the boat and himself. Webb
promptly removed his hat, handkerchief, coat, and
all his clothing, save a pair of short red cotton
trunks around his loins, and without a word of
farewell, plunged boldly into the water at a point
opposite the Maid of the Mist landing. A moment
later he rose gracefully to the surface, and swimming with infinite ease and power, struck boldly
out. It was 4:24 o'clock, New York time, when
he dived into the river, which seemed to be flowing

placidly onward, giving on its surface few indications of the awful dangers beyond. He cleared the water with strong and steady strokes, swimming on his breast with his head clear from the surface. He kept in the center of the stream, and the strong eddies, which occasionally swirled past him, seemed in no way to impede or swerve him from his course. As he approached the old suspension bridge the flow of the current increased with remarkable rapidity. There were about two hundred spectators on the bridge who saw the intrepid swimmer glide toward them, pass swiftly beneath them, and ere they could reach the east side of the structure he was fifty yards down the current. He was carried along as fast as the eye could follow him. With speechless wonder and fear he was seen to reach the first furious billows of the rapids. Onward he swept like a feather in the sea. High on the crest of a huge boulder of water his head and shoulders gleamed for an instant and then was lost in a dark abyss of turmoiling water. Again he appeared, his arms steadily moving as if balancing himself for a plunge into another mighty wave. The tumbling, rushing, swirling element seemed to give forth an angry, sullen roar, as if sounding the death knell of the ill-fated swimmer. Once more away down the rapids he was seen still apparently braving fate and stemming the seething waters with marvelous skill and endurance. Instead of being hurled hither and thither, as might have been expected, he was carried with furious rapidity onward, almost in a strait course.

For nearly a mile he was hurried forward by the tumultuous rushing waters, and still he seemed to be riding the awful billows in safety. In four minutes after he had passed under the old suspension bridge he had been hurried through the terrible rapids and arrived at the mouth of the great whirlpool. Reaching what seemed to be less troubled and dangerous waters he raised his head well above the surface, gazed for an instant toward the American shore, and then turned his face to the high bluff on the Canadian side. A second later he dived or sank and was seen no more. There were very few who witnessed the tragic disappearance, as the passage was completed in an almost incomprehensibly brief period. Mr. Kyle and a few others were on the banks of the whirlpool below the cliff, but they waited and watched in vain for the foolhardy victim of the perilous and, as it doubtless proved, fatal venture to reappear.

There can be very little doubt that he was drawn down into one of the powerful eddies or under currents, or into the down swirl of the central whirlpool, and was too exhausted to struggle from the deadly embrace. Two ladies and an enterprising Canadian reporter aver that they saw him fairly in the current of the whirlpool, but the general testimony is that he did not appear above the surface after he sank or dived at the mouth of the maelstrom.

HOW CAPTAIN WEBB WAS KILLED.

The post-mortem examination of Captain Webb's body was made at Lockport Sunday afternoon by Drs. Edward Smith, of Lewiston ; M. S. Lang, of Suspension Bridge, and C. N. Palmer, of Lockport. They found the body in an active state of decomposition, but no bones were broken and none of the injuries except the wound three and one-half inches long in the cranium were sufficient to cause death. The cranium wound they decided was produced after death. All the blood presented a distinctly red color, showing that it was not deoxidized by asphyxia in drowning, but that death ensued prior to that condition. None of the characteristic symptoms of death by drowning were present, nor was there any local injury sufficient to cause death. It was therefore concluded that death resulted from the shock from the reactionary force of the water in the whirlpool rapids coming in contact with the submerged body with such force as to instantly destroy the respiratory power, and, in fact, all vital action, by direct pressure from the force of contact. The shock was of sufficient intensity as to paralyze the nerve centers, partially dessicate the muscular tissues, and forestall death by drowning. The conclusion was therefore reached that no living body can, or ever will, pass through the rapids alive. The river bed at the whirlpool rapids is much narrowed, and suddenly assumes great precipitancy. The water strikes the unyielding banks with great violence, and by reaction meets with such resistance as to form in the center a mountainous ridge of encroaching waters from twenty to thirty feet in height. Into this Captain Webb was submerged after passing the first breaker, and instantly subjected to the immense pressure indicated upon his body. This caused his death.

In speaking the other night with some friends of the perils of the pearl divers and their encounters with the ground sharks of the ocean, an old soldier was present, who, after listening to our several stories of the monsters of the deep, related the following, which will possess interest for those who love the marvelous, and I preserved it, or as much of it as I could recollect, for a place in my diary. The old veteran styled it—

A DREADFUL NIGHT.

"In the vicinity of the barracks assigned to the European soldiers in India, there are usually a number of little solitary buildings or cells, where the more disorderly members of the corps are confined for longer or shorter terms, by order of the commanding officer. In one of these, on a certain occasion, was locked up poor Jock Hall, a Scotsman belonging to Edinburgh or Leith. Jock had got intoxicated, and being found in that position at the hour of drill, was sentenced to eight days' solitary imprisonment.

"Soldiers in India have their bedding partly furnished by the honorable company, and find the remainder for themselves. About this part of house furnishing, however, Jock Hall troubled himself very little, being one of those hardy, reckless beings on whom privation and suffering seem to make no impression. A hard floor was as good as a down bed to Jock; and, therefore, as he never scrupled to sell what he got, it may be supposed that his sleeping furniture was none of the most abundant or select. Such as it was, he was stretched upon and under it one night in his cell, during his term of penance, and possibly was reflecting on the impropriety of in future putting 'an enemy into his mouth to steal away his brains,' when, lo! he thought he heard a rustling in his cell, close by him.

"At this moment he recollected that he had not, as he ought to have done, stopped up an air hole, which entered the cell on a level with its floor, and also with the rock, externally, on which the building was planted. A strong suspicion of what had happened, or was about to happen, came over Hall's mind; but he probably knew it was too late to do any good, could he even find the hole in the darkness, and get it closed. He, therefore, lay still, and in a minute or two heard another rustle close to him, which was followed by the cold, slimy touch of a snake upon his bare foot! Who in such a situation would not have started and bawled for help? Jock did neither; he lay stone still and held his peace, knowing that his cries would most probably have been unheard by the distant guard. Had his bed-clothes been more plentiful, he might have endeavored to protect himself by wrapping them closely around him, but this their scantiness forbade. Accordingly, being aware that, although a motion or touch will provoke snakes to bite, they will not generally do it without such excitement, Jock held himself as still as if he had been a log. Meanwhile, his horrible bed-fellow, which he at once felt to be of great size, crept over his feet, legs and body, and, lastly, over his very face. Nothing but the most astonishing firmness of nerve, and the consciousness that the moving of muscle would have signed his death warrant, could have enabled the poor fellow to undergo this dreadful trial. For a whole hour did the reptile crawl backward and forward over Jock's body and face, as if satisfying itself, seemingly, that it had nothing to fear from the recumbent object on its own part. At length it took up a position somewhere about his head, and went to rest in apparent security.

"The poor soldier's trial, however, was not over. Till daylight he remained in the same posture, flat on his back, without daring to stir a limb, from the fear of disturbing his dangerous companion. Never, perhaps, was dawn so anxiously longed for by mortal man. When it did come, Jock cautiously looked about him, arose noiselessly, and moved over to the corner of his cell, where there lay a pretty large stone. This he seized, and looked about for his intruder. Not seeing the snake, be became assured that it was under his pillow. He raised the end of this just sufficiently to get a peep of the creature's crest. Jock then pressed his knee firmly on the pillow, but allowed the snake to wriggle out his head, which he battered to pieces with the stone. This done, the courageous fellow for the first time breathed freely. When the hour for breakfast came, Jock, who thought little about the matter after it was fairly over, took the opportunity of the opening of the door to throw the snake out.

"When the officer whose duty it was to visit the cells for the day was going his rounds, he perceived a crowd round the cell door examining the reptile, which was described by the natives as of the most venomous character, its bite being invariably and rapidly mortal. The officer, on being told that it had been killed by a man in the adjoining cell, went in, and inquired into the matter. 'When did you first know that there was a snake in the cell with you?' said he. 'About 9 o'clock last night,' was Jock's reply. 'Why didn't you call to the guard?' asked the officer. 'I thought the guard wadna hear me, and I was feared I might tramp on't, so I just lay still.' 'But you might have been bit. Did you know that you would have died instantly?' 'I kent that very weel,' said Jock, 'but they say that snakes winna meddle with you, if you dinna meddle with them; sae I just let it crawl as it liket.' 'Well, my lad, I believe you did what was best, after all; but it was not what one man in a thousand could have done.'

"When the story was told, and the snake shown to the commanding officer, he thought the same; and Jock, for his extraordinary nerve and courage, got a remission of his punishment. For some time, at least, he took care how he again got into such a situation as to expose himself to the chance of passing another night with such a bed-fellow."

After the telling of this story by the old soldier we had many questions to ask him about the life of the Scotchman and what became of him. We all agreed that it was a thrilling narrative, and had some further conversation in regard to the poisonous reptiles of India.

THE SNAKE STORY.

Our attention was now directed to an old Virginian, an ex-Confederate, who evidently wished to say something, and we asked him if he could not relate us a serpentine yarn. "Well, yes, I can," said the Virginian :

"You see," said he, " I was a great rebel, and I resolved at the commencement of the war to join the Southern army and never surrender to the hated Yanks. I was in the first battle of Bull Run, which I honestly thought at the time had closed the war, but I found out my mistake in fully fifty battles afterward. Well, I fought on and on until we came to Appomattox, where General Lee concluded he would surrender, and I concluded I wouldn't. I mounted a large mule, which I took from a Confederate wagon-train and fled toward Texas. After many hardships I reached the Rio Grande and crossed into Mexico. I got a bite to eat at Matamoras and started for the interior. I was traveling along one day, nursing my wrath against the Yanks, when I espied a beautiful lot of flowers. I was always fond of flowers, and I dismounted and stepped aside for a moment to admire a rich turf of large, red blossoms, my mule having plodded on about

9.

eight or ten yards ahead, when, as I turned from the flowers toward the path, a sensation as of a flash of lightning struck my sight, and I saw a brilliant and powerful snake winding its coils around the head and body of my poor mule. It was a large and magnificent boa of a black and yellow color, and it had entwined the poor beast so firmly in its folds that ere he had time to utter more than one feeble bray he was crushed and dead, and I just caught a glimpse of his ears, bidding farewell to a vain world as they disappeared down the throat of the snake. The perspiration broke out on my forehead as I thought of my own narrow escape, and only remaining a moment to view the movements of the monster as he wiped his mouth with his tail, I rushed through the brush-wood, swam the Rio Grande, and didn't stop running until I got back to Virginia, where I immediately registered and have voted the Republican ticket ever since.''

THE DOG STORY.

Speaking of your run back to Virginia from Mexico, said a Yankee in the crowd, and of the great snake swallowing your mule, reminds me of my own adventures. I, too, was a soldier, but belonged to the Federal army, and a poor dog that I captured the last day of the war caused me to be driven out of Egypt. After my discharge from the army I was paid off, and calling my dog I hastened homeward, the dog at my heels. In a few days after reaching home the dog grew unpopular with the family, and having a strong desire for adventure, I concluded to leave home, taking my dog along. The viceroy of Egypt was then in need of soldiers, and meeting a crowd of convivial spirits we concluded to sail for Egypt and offer our services to Abas Pasha, who was then ruler of the land. His memory now is held in universal detestation. To him fell all the vices, with none of the redeeming virtues, of the illustrious Mohammed Ali. The guide conducts the traveler to the room where Abas, at once the Nero and Caligula of Egypt, is supposed to have been strangled by the two Circassian guards whom he always kept standing by his bedside during his sleeping hours.

The Pasha while viceroy visited Alexandria twice, but could not be induced to approach the city afterward from a superstitious idea that the third visit would prove fatal to him.

He refused our application for enlistment in his service on the ground that his troubles were almost at an end, and he did not need any more troops. I was now almost in despair. I had nothing left to love me but that little dog of mine, and he was crying for bread. The dog, however, proved almost a fortune to me, as the sequel will show.

The Pasha's favorite occupation was to make large collections of dogs and cats, animals which he cherished much as the ancient sovereigns of Egypt did apes and ibis. The lares and penates of Abas Pasha were quartered in different parts of Egypt, where they enjoyed his periodical visits. After the death of the Pasha, however, these canine and feline recipients of the royal favor were turned loose, and are now the most pitiable of objects. Well, on a certain day I appeared on the streets of Cairo leading my dog possessed of two tails. Information of this rare phenomenon was conveyed to Abas Pasha, and I was fortunate enough to be at once summoned to wait upon his highness at the palace. I was frightened to death for fear of exposure, but the Pasha was in ecstacies. The *apotheosis* of Anubis, after having exhausted the

cycle of the metempsychosis, and appeared again
in his original form, could not have given him
greater delight.   I declared I would not part with
the creature for less than twelve thousand five
hundred Turkish piasters, $500, a sum which the
Pasha at last consented to give, not suspecting for
a moment that the extra tail was the product of
Yankee ingenuity.

The latter tail became disengaged the same evening while the Pasha of two tails was exhibiting his
paragon of canine wonders to a circle of admiring
friends.   Abas was infuriated.   Of course I was
nowhere to be found.   On receiving the money I
had fled.   Hiring a boat at an enormous sum I had
left Cairo in the distance never to return.   I bid
adieu to Egypt—the blessed of sunny skies—and
all the delights of the great-eyed Orient.   I did
not feel safe until I stood beneath the folds of the
star-spangled banner, the flag of the free, where
no Pasha could molest me.

I have some of that dog money left yet, boys, and
I intend to settle in Virginia and invest in an oyster patch, and vote the straight Democratic ticket,
and that is how I came to be prospecting in Virginia.

ABOUT SHARKS.

I received a letter from a friend asking me for
information touching the "man-eating propensities
of the shark," and asks: "Will sharks attack a man
in the water?"

It is a common belief among sailors that among
the different species there is one, known as the
"ground shark," which differs from his more active and sport-loving brothers, and will "attack a
man in the water."

In support of the fact that this belief is not a superstition, I will relate the following fact :

Some time in the summer of 1872, when the crew of the United States steamer Kearsarge were bathing in the waters of Algiricas bay, opposite Gibraltar, one of this species was observed to rise to the surface, moved toward one of the swimmers, who splashed the water about him considerably, and from this or some unknown cause the shark changed his course and attacked another man. The man swam away and called for help, but before the boat, which was lowered and ready to rescue any who should need aid, could reach the swimmer, the shark turned on his back, opened his capacious jaw, darted forward, and, seizing his victim by the body just below one arm, slowly descended to his slimy bed.

The boat arrived at the spot where the finny monster and his victim sank, only to see them disappear in the manner described.

It is well known that the inhabitants of the coast in tropical countries have little fear of the shark, and expert swimmers can manage to kill them with a sharp weapon. Perhaps the man-eater of Algiricas bay might have been beaten off by a swimmer skilled in such warfare.

If an expert swimmer should be attacked by a shark, the shark could be easily disposed of with a stiletto, which they always carry with them. Should more than one shark take a fancy to dine on a poor fellow he would have a busy time to escape the monsters. But taken singly they are very slow in their movements and can be easily dispatched. One came in very close proximity to me once on a swim from Fortress Monroe to Ocean View. On seeing the shark approaching me, as I thought, I drew my dagger, and in doing so cut my arm. I

wounded myself in the commencement, and would
go into a battle at a disadvantage, but much to my
relief it sank out of sight into the sea. You may
rest assured that for some time afterward I kept a
sharp look-out for my wide-mouthed friend. But
I never saw him again.

It is not a very pleasant sensation, however,
when miles from the shore, swimming along, to
fancy that a shark is near, and you are in danger
of becoming the bait of one. My experience is
that they are very scarce in our waters, and harmless.
The land sharks in our cities are most to be dreaded—
those that feed upon your purse and good nature—
who catch you by honeyed names, who are convivial
over the cups when you pay for the wine ; who
pronounce you a good fellow so long as your money
lasts, and denounce you as a fraud when it is all
gone. Oh, no, the sharks of the ocean harm very
few souls, but the sharks of the land, they are
most to be dreaded ; for they swallow you up so
gradually that it is very pleasant to be swallowed,
but awake to find that we have gone down rather too
deep in the throat of the monster to ever escape
with any reputation or "loose change" left.

VAMPIRES.

Speaking of sharks reminds me of a description
of a naval officer. He wrote me, "I have this day
seen a real live vampire." He describes the reptile
as follows: "So many horrible associations of
blood and terror are connected with the popular
ideas of this extraordinary animal that when it
was known that one had actually arrived, a most
intense desire was manifested to obtain a peep at
it, and accordingly the vessel was crowded during
the day by hosts of curious visitors until its re-

moval. It was of the Sumatran species, and the first
living specimen ever seen in America. It was
of the most horrible aspect, and well deserves the
name, remaining constantly suspended to the
roof of his cage by immense hooks at the edges of
the wings, his head ·hanging downward, and his
eyes glistening with most vivid brightness.

"The vampire will attack horses, mules, asses,
horned cattle, and the crest of fowls, which generally die in consequence, as gangrene is engendered
in the wounds. Even man is not secure from these
insidious assaults. I can bear testimony, having
had the ends of my toes phlebotomized gratis by
this nocturnal surgeon while sleeping in a cottage
in the open country. The wound is not felt at
the time of its infliction, as the blood is withdrawn
by the most gentle suction, entirely from the capil-
lary vessel of the skin, and not from any of the
veins or arteries, and the victim is besides lulled into
a deep slumber by the flapping of his destroyer's
wings, who thus enjoys his banquet undisturbed."

THE PRESS.

The stranger coming to Washington, especially
if he stops at one of our large hotels and is convivial in his habits, will soon form the acquaintance of the jolly Bohemian, who is ever on the alert
for news—the hotel arrival being an important
item. No jollier set ever roamed a forest or enjoyed the hospitality of a city. They are a privil-
eged class, have the entré everywhere, and are
treated with the utmost respect. They occupy the
chairs in the front rows at the grand opera and
theatrical performances without money and without price. A line of commendation of the performance and a little taffy for the manager is all that

is required in return. Actors and actresses smile upon the squad of Bohemians in the most fascinating style, and the *Star, Republican, Post* and *Critic* acknowledge the smile the day after in a complimentary paragraph, " the rival of Charlotte Cushman in Meg Merilles is at the National," or " the equal of the elder Booth struts the broad stage at Albaugh's in the grandest tragedies of the Bard of Avon."

The new Congressman naturally takes to the Bohemian. A word, a line, a paragraph even, is his, if his conduct is such as to win the esteem of the jolly fellow who makes and unmakes Congressmen; who gives the public man his reputation even if he has none before, and robs him of it even if he comes to Washington with one, but happens to offend the newspaper man by refusing to administer spiritual consolation to the representatives of the press.

It is a part of wisdom in the public functionary to cultivate friendly feelings with the jolly Bohemians. They all think alike; they go in flocks like blackbirds, will commend in a chorus, and damn you, and surround you, blast all your public expectations, and leave you a degraded being on the earth. Such is the power of printers' ink; such is the temper of those who—

> "As they journey through life
> Live by the way,"

on the wine and the fat of the land.

This is one class of Bohemians, but the better we will now mention. The word of itself signifies a roving, shiftless disposition, but as applied to newspaperdom it has a different meaning. Some of the brightest intellects of the country belong to the tribe, and the most distinguished orators and statesmen of our day were at some period of their lives members of the press, and owe their political advancement to the position they occupied on the same.

The Bohemian sports around the foot of the ladder that leads to fame. He can easily climb if he possesses the brain power, the ability to achieve greatness. The press is the mouth of the public, and the Bohemian puts in and shapes the utterances. What is "read in the papers" forms public opinion, and the Bohemian is the director.

Is it any wonder then that the class is allowed privileges and immunities enjoyed by no other? The people look to the press as the great lever that moves the world ; but without the Bohemian, what would be the press?

There are many men of many minds, and it takes a diversity of talent to run a newspaper. The sober and staid intellect required of an editor would be out of place in the Washington correspondent who writes in a serio-comic style, and takes life as he finds it, with a pleasant word for everybody, and his lips ever ready to say "come up" to a dry acquaintance when he has a quarter. They, as a class, are a merry, jovial lot, happy as the days are long, and possess the good will of the public.

I know a great number of journalists sojourning in Washington, and a jolly crowd they are. I am indebted for many a good "send off" from Bohemians. Among my many friends of the press is one John McCarthy, of the Baltimore *Sun* and New York *Herald*. John is a great temperance man, and tells temperance stories with a merry twinkle in his eye, but never smiles ; John knows better than smile, or take a smile. He believes in giving a drunkard all the whisky he can drink until he is killed, and then the community should care for the widow and children of the deceased. John would

come around to my Natatorium and give me a
lecture on temperance about three times a week
regularly ; he is one of the most companionable
fellows I ever knew, is this same dry John Mc-
Carthy.

———   •

CHAPTER IX.

THE SWIMMING DRILL.

(A practical treatise on the art of swimming by Robert Emmet
Odlum, professor of swimming, Washington, D. C., 1885.)

PREFACE.

I have for a long time intended to publish a book
on physical exercise, and also to issue a swimming
manual, so that persons might be taught that useful art on land. Companies and regiments are
drilled by tactics, and I can see no reason why tactics could not be applied to swimming and taught
even in our public schools. If the teacher was
competent, and the pupil understood his lesson, he
would be "at home on the billow," if accident
should overtake him, or be educated to enjoy the
luxury of a swim whenever he thought proper to
do so, without the fear of being drowned. It has
been contended that all military organizations
should be taught to swim, and to enable all persons to embrace the opportunity to learn the useful
art, I have prepared and tender the public "a swimming drill," illustrated.

All four-footed animals swim a few days after
they are born, the reason being that their mode of
progress in water is similar to their mode of pro-

gress on land, and, therefore, natural to them; but with man certain unnatural motions of the legs, aided by others of the arms, not at all required for progression on land, are needed to keep him on the surface of the water, and this artificial method of progression must be acquired to enable him to swim. To teach the necessary motions is the object of this work, and if they are thoroughly acquired there is no reason why man should not be able, like animals, to swim the first time he goes into the water.

Very few books on the subject of swimming have ever been issued, which is rather remarkable. The Athenians looked with contempt upon the person who did not possess the art, and when they wished to speak in terms of derision of any man, they would say, "he doesn't even know how to swim." I am confident the "swimming drill" will fill a long-felt want, and by close attention to its contents many will learn to swim.

It is absolutely necessary that some, and very beneficial that most, men in an army should be able to swim; every endeavor ought, therefore, to be made to teach this art.

For civilians of all classes and both sexes the following exercises will be found exceedingly useful, as they combine setting-up drill, the preliminary balance step taught at dancing lessons, and swimming motions; and it is evident after learning these motions people are more likely to have some idea of swimming in case of sudden accidental immersion; at any rate, they would become familiar with the few strokes necessary to place them out of danger, and therefore on that plea alone they are strongly recommended.

The remarks on the practical uses of swimming apply chiefly to soldiers, but they will be found valuable to any one, more especially, perhaps, to the ever-increasing number of persons who yearly travel.

In the recent report of the Adjutant-General of the Army, giving a statistical exhibit of deaths in the United States Army during the war, it is shown that 4,844 soldiers were drowned.

Commodore Walker, of the United States Navy, in a recent interview said that few sailors in the navy could swim. In all his experience he never knew one that could swim. Comment is unnecessary.

Appalling statement.—I find from a statement made by the committee of the British and Foreign Sailors' Society in 1839 it appears that within the short period of four months and three days previous to April last, there had been wrecked one hundred and sixty vessel—all of whose crews had perished. Averaging the crew of each ship at ten, will give a loss of one thousand and six hundred lives. It is further shown that of vessels stranded, foundered, abandoned, not heard of, &c., within the same period, the number of vessels affected by such catastrophes is 576. If only one soul has perished from each of the vessels which have suffered from the above contingencies, we number a loss of five hundred and seventy-six lives. Then add to these four hundred and twenty-four certainly known to have perished, and we have a total from all causes of at least two thousand and six hundred lives— on an average something more than twenty-one every day during the period of four short months.

EXERCISE ON LAND.

PART I.—PRELIMINARY EXERCISE.

The men are drawn up in line at three paces interval.

The instructor gives the word of command:

Exercise of right arm and leg—one—two—three.

Fig. 1.   Fig. 2.

On the command "one" the men draw the right foot up into the hollow of the left knee, the toe pointing outward and downward, the right elbow close to the side, the fore-arm held perpendicularly upward, the hand open, the fingers extended and touching each other, the palm of the hand inward. [Fig. 1.]

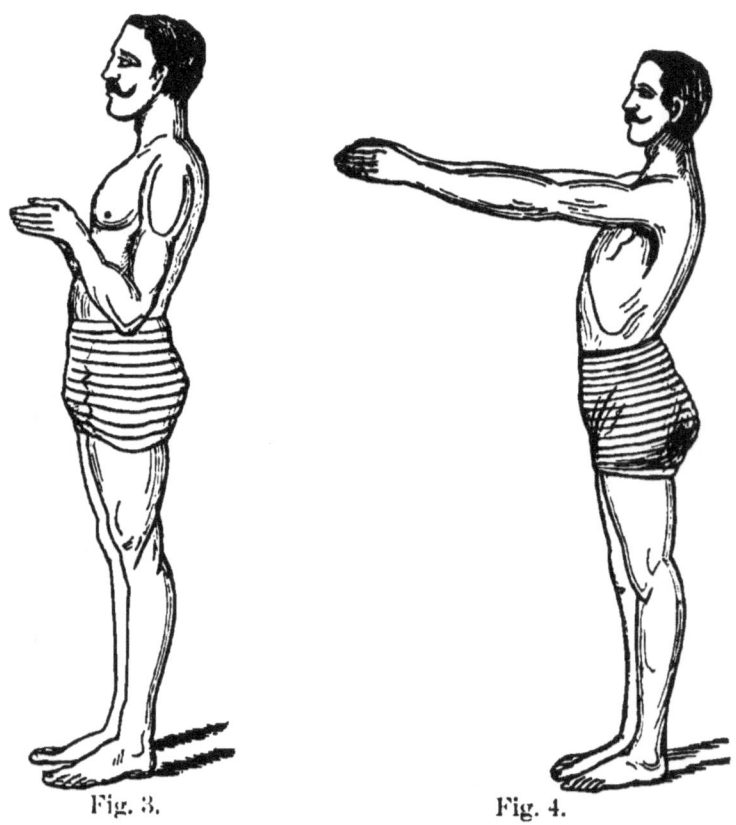

Fig. 3.   Fig. 4.

On the command "two" then extend the arm upward and the leg downward quickly and simultaneously, the latter being shot out to the right. [Fig. 2.]

On the command "three" close the legs, and lower the hand to the side, returning to the first position, and so continue till ordered to halt, counting each motion. The same exercise can then be done by standing on the right leg and working the left arm and leg.

PART II.—SWIMMING MOTIONS.

Exercise of the arms.

The men are drawn up as before.

The instructor gives the command :

First Swimming Practice: Arm Motion—one—two—three—four.

On the command "one" draw the elbows into the side, lay the palms of the hands together, fingers extended to the front, and touching each other. [Fig. 3.]

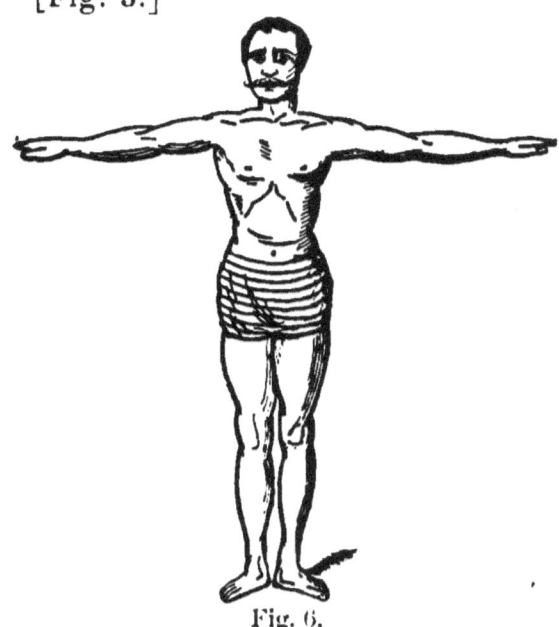

Fig. 6.

On the command "two" shoot the arms out straight, the hands remaining together. [Fig. 4.]

At "three" separate the hands about six inches, palms of the hands downward, and slightly inward. [Fig. 5.]

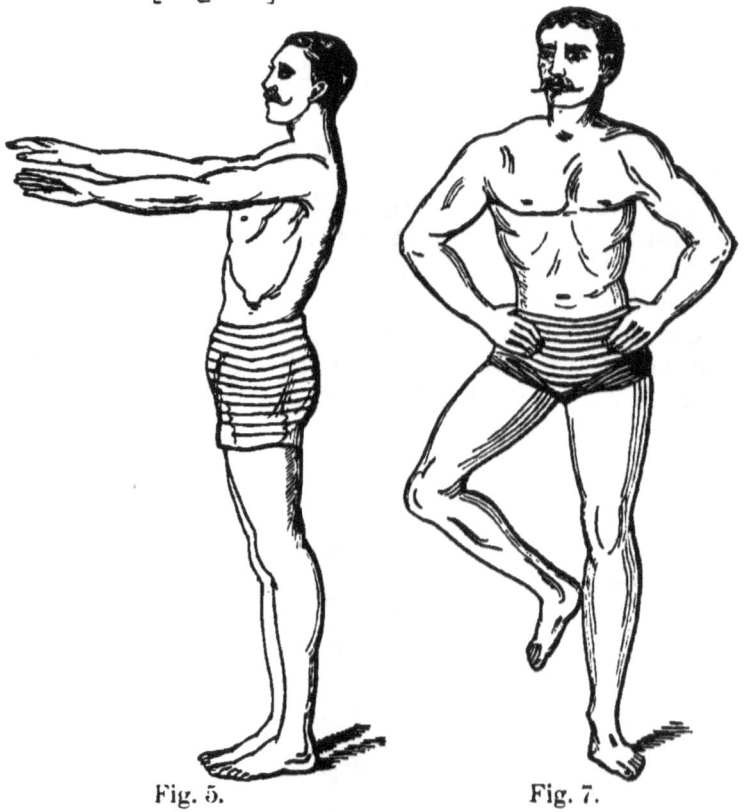

Fig. 5.   Fig. 7.

At "four" slowly describe a half circle with extended arms and bring the elbows down to the side; return to the first position, counting each motion. [Fig. 6.]

Exercise of the legs.

The men drawn up as before, place their hands on their hips, fingers in front, and thumbs behind.

The instructor gives the word of command:

Second Swimming Practice: Leg Motions—right foot—one—two—three.

On the command "one" raise the right heel into hollow of left leg, bending the knee as much as possible, toes pointing outward. [Fig. 7.]

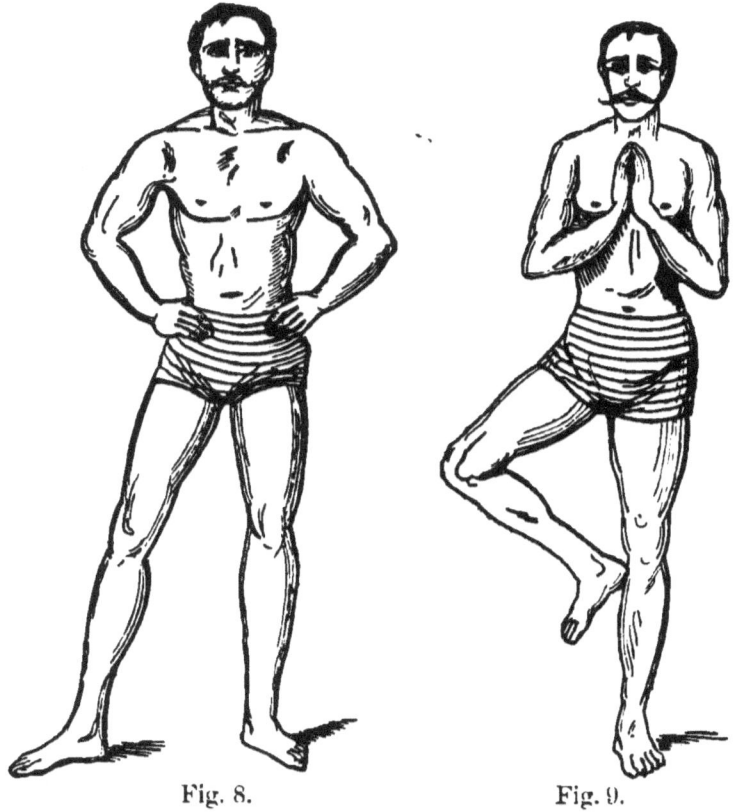

Fig. 8.   Fig. 9.

At "two" extend the right leg quickly to the right. [Fig. 8.]

At "three" draw in the right leg to the left. Repeat with the left leg.

Exercise of arm and leg.

The instructor gives the word of command:
Third Swimming Practice: Arm and Leg Motions—right leg—one—two—three.

On the command "one" the arms and right leg are brought into position as in first and second practice, above explained. [Fig. 9.]

At "two" the arms are extended, the leg at the same time being straightened. [Fig. 10.]

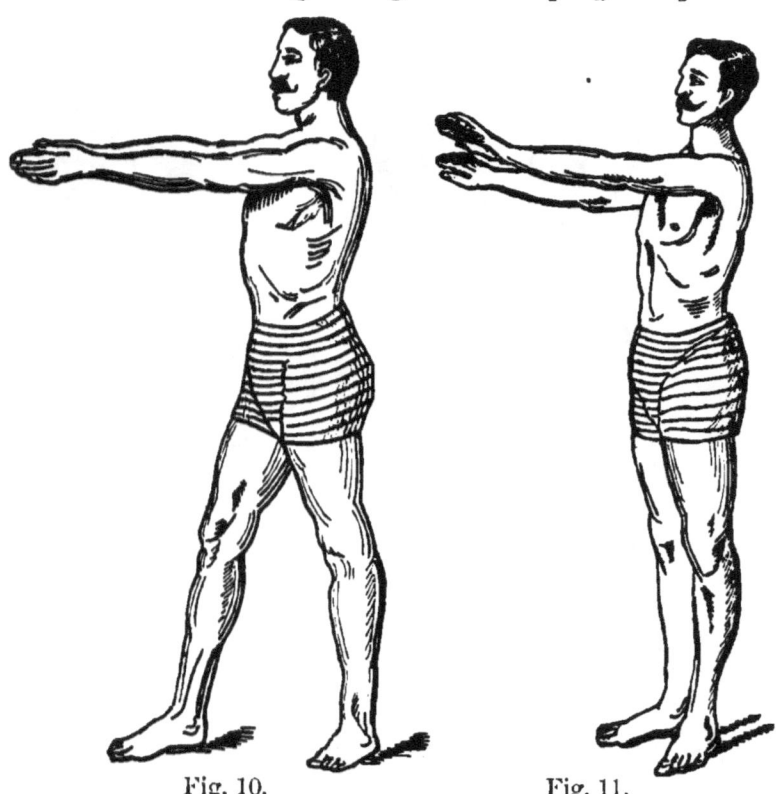

Fig. 10.   Fig. 11.

At "three" the extended leg is drawn up to the other one, and the hands separated about six inches, palms downward, the outside edges slightly raised. [Fig. 11.]

At "four" the hands slowly describe half circle with straightened arms. Then the elbow is drawn into the side, palms of the hands together, the heel raised toward the leg, resuming the first position, counting all motions. [Fig. 12.]

Fig. 12.

We cannot too strongly recommend these practices to any one wishing to learn swimming quickly.

PART III.—DESCRIPTION OF SWIMMING MOTIONS ON A BENCH.

The men lay flat on the bench or lean over a plank or table.

The instructor gives the word of command:
Swimming Practice—one—two—three—four.

On command "one" the men draw up the heels,
bending the knees as much as possible, keeping the
heels together, the toes pointing outward, the elbows by the side, the palms of the hands together,
the fingers straight and pointing to the front, the
head slightly bent back.   [Fig. 13.]

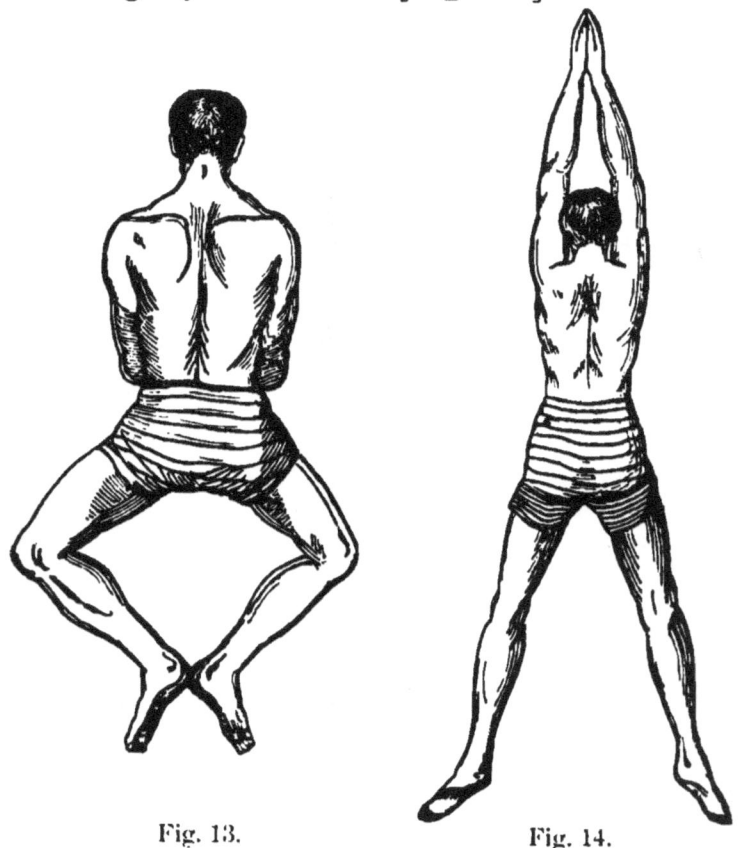

Fig. 13.   Fig. 14.

On the command "two" they extend the arms
and legs smartly, separating the latter at same time.
[Fig. 14.]

At " three" close the legs and separate the hands about six inches, palms down and turned outward. [Fig. 15.]

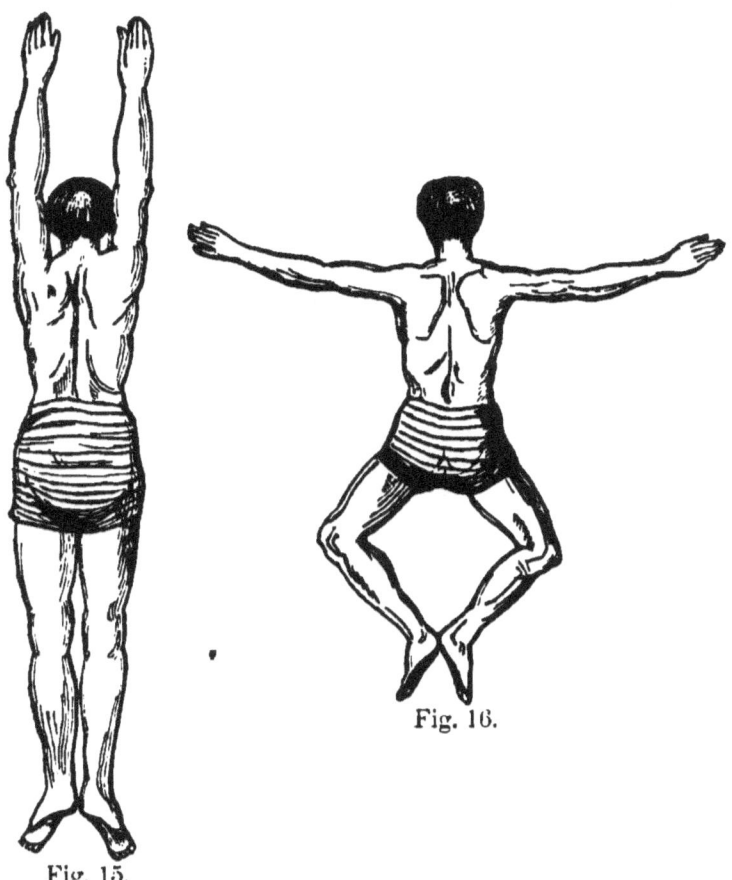

Fig. 15.

Fig. 16.

At " four" slowly describe a half circle with both hands and extended arms, then close the elbows to the body, draw up the heels, and return to the first position, counting each motion.   [Fig. 16.]

Exercises in the water.

First. Each man supported by a girdle and rope repeats the exercise he has learned on the stool ; he is then allowed to move forward, the rope being slackened gradually until he is in reality swimming unaided.

Second. The man must be taught to float in order to rest himself. To do this he must turn over on his back, stretch out the legs, and make a horizontal motion with the hands.

In order to progress in this position he must draw up his heels, turning out his knees as much as possible, and strike out against the water, closing the legs sharply at the end of the stroke, which gives extra impetus by the legs closing on the wedge of water they contain.

Third. It is important that men should be taught to dive. They must first be accustomed to keep their heads under water as long as possible, and keep their eyes open in this position.

In diving, a man springs in head first and swims about on the bottom.

To return to the surface he most stand up on the bottom, give a good push off, and if necessary swim upward.

Men must also be taught to jump in feet first, taking a good run, the head and upper part of the body leaning rather back, the legs close together, and arms by the side.

General remarks.

The swimming lessons should take place in the morning after the rising of the sun, and at least an hour before sunset.

Men should be careful not to go into the water

whilst the body is in a state of perspiration, and *to first wet the head.* They should not come out before they are tired, and should then dry themselves quickly, dress and move about.

Bathing must be avoided on a full stomach. When the place admits of it, a row of pickets must be driven both up and down stream to mark the places which are out of depth.

In bathing in public places, or indeed anywhere, bathing drawers should be worn. These can be formed of a handkerchief folded into three corners, two tied round the waist and the third brought up between the legs and tied to the girdle formed by the two first.

Hints for teaching swimming.

In order that these lessons should have the best results, it is necessary that they should be continued without interruption, and that they should take place, especially at first, at least twice a week, if possible three times. Experience has proved that two or three lessons taken at short intervals are of more value than five or six with longer periods intervening ; in the latter case not only do men forget what they have already learned, but also lose any extra confidence they may have acquired during the preceding lesson.

It is found that from eight to ten lessons suffice to overcome the preliminary difficulties, and to bring men to the point where they can practice the art by themselves. This step once made, the rest is a mere matter of improvement, and comes with practice.

Squads should be divided into three classes ; each lesson for beginners forming the third class should last from twenty to twenty-five minutes.

The second class, or those who can get on without the aid of the rope, can manage half an hour, whilst three-quarters of an hour is not found too much for those who can swim freely, and who employ the time in perfecting and improving themselves.

Out of a battalion of 600 men, 450 to 500 could learn swimming. They would require two lessons a week, and 180 to 200 men would have to be taught daily; this might easily be done, the size of the squads and the number of instructions being regulated according to circumstances, probably by the size of the bathing place.

Regulations.

1. Men to be divided into three classes.
2. All men in the first class to be thoroughly up in the exercises on land and water.
3. The men of the second class will first bathe with a girdle and rope, and pass on to being supported by the pole, until by degrees they can dispense with all aid, swimming alone. (But to give the pupil every confidence, the instructor can hold over him the end of a pole, to be grasped as soon as he feels tired.)
4. The men of the third class will wear the rope and girdle, by which the instructor can support them whilst giving a lesson.

The rope for the second class can be made simply as follows: A long rope, buoyed at intervals with corks, has a piece spliced in at about two inches from one end, thus forming a double end, about the width of a man's shoulders; at the extremities of these ends are loops into which the arms are to be placed.

5. The first class, on appointed days once or twice a week, must be practiced in saving life,

crossing rivers with and without arms and ammunition.

6. The duration of lessons for third or fourth classes must not exceed twenty minutes or half an hour; of the second class three-quarters of an hour, and the first class one hour.

7. If the bathing place admits of it, it is a good plan to teach men to swim horses, at first dismounted and holding the bridle, and afterward mounted as well as bridled.   *

8. Men who are very hot must be careful not to go into the bath till they are thoroughly cool, and bathing must be strictly prohibited to any one who has just eaten or drunk a great deal; three hours should intervene between a meal and bathing lesson.

The uses of swimming to a soldier.

1. To extricate himself from danger, which may occur from any accident.

2. To help another similarly situated.

3. To cross a swift and deep stream without any help, and to take his arms, ammunition and accouterments with him, which is often of great service in war time. It is, therefore, important that the first class should be practiced in these things.

To extricate one's self in case of accident.

To swim well is often of great service to men suddenly falling in the water; a man who can only swim a little feels his power of buoyancy negatived by having his clothes, &c., on. He calls out, sinks, and not being able to dive, fear and the suddenness of the case make him lose his head; from that moment he no longer goes through the swimming motions and is soon insensible.

To guard against such cases, all men of the first class should be practiced at swimming, first in their clothes and afterward in full equipment, till they have lost all fear ; and eventually with weapons, infantry men carrying their knapsacks on their backs, and the cavalry men their swords by their sides.

The first thing to be done as soon as an infantry man thinks he is sinking, is to cast off his rifle and throw it away, and extricate himself from his pack, of which the straps over his shoulders have been loosened beforehand, in order more easily to free his arms if necessary. Then with a strong push of his legs he will try to regain the surface, take breath, and as quickly as possible reach a place of safety, taking care not to hurry too much, and thereby lose strength.

To help a sinking man.

Most people in danger lose their heads, their movements are vague, and calculated rather to drown them than otherwise. They instinctively grasp at everything, and whatever they get hold of they cling to so perniciously that it is next to impossible to get them to let go ; therefore, to save a drowning man he must be approached with the greatest care. The following is a good plan : Free yourself of clothes and approach him from up-stream, wait till his back is turned, then seize him suddenly and firmly with both hands under the shoulders, keeping him at arm's length, thus supporting him in such a manner that his head is above water, push him toward a place of safety. In case you become very tired, or the drowning man turns round, let him go, and as soon as a favorable opportunity occurs seize him again, and make for the shore; if he is a stronger man than you it may be necessary to wait till he becomes insensible before approaching him, for if once gripped by a drowning man it is a matter of great difficulty, and requires all one's self possession to get free. Should such a contingency unfortunately occur, take breath, bring the fingers of both hands under the extremities of the hands of the man who has seized you, by strong effort at the same moment freeing yourself with a kick; get quickly out of his way and wait about for a favorable moment to seize the man again.

Crossing a river with arms and ammunition.

This accomplishment can be done in several ways. Arms and ammunition can be pushed across in floating baskets, or the man can carry them himself; the latter is always difficult, and only to be done by men well trained. As a general rule it must be remembered that the swimmer under these circumstances has not free use of his arms and legs, so that what movements he can make with these limbs should be of the best. It is clear that his load should be in equilibrium with the mass of water which he displaces. Whenever it is possible to obtain anything light to form rafts they must be constructed in sufficient number to keep the clothes, arms and ammunition dry; the latter for greater safety should be put in buckets or casks. A rope is fastened to this raft, a ring at the end of which is fastened to the man who, swimming in front, thus drags it to the opposite bank. If the rafts can carry the effects of several men, two or more can pull in front and others push behind.

The following is the quickest and safest way of

crossing a stream, taking over at the same time one's arms, &c.: In the case of an infantry man, he must free himself of his cloak, belt, and knapsack, and unbuckle the strap of his rifle.

On entering the water he must put one or two packets of cartridges in his shako, helmet, or cap, which he must buckle on tightly, then holding rifle horizontally, the barrel downward, the lock upward, the butt slightly higher than the barrel, he places his head in the ring of the rope; the rifle lays balanced obliquely over the man's shoulder, the lock somewhat over the neck, the stock immediately over the left shoulder blade out of the way. The bayonet can be put on the rifle or stuck in the belt. Thus equipped the man takes the water, walking carefully along until he gets out of his depth, and then quickly and in a slightly bent position he begins to swim, getting as much as possible out of each motion, without trying to cross too quickly, or he will tire himself. If many men are crossing at the same time they must take care not to get too near each other, or jostle one another.

CHAPTER X.

THE LEAP FROM THE BROOKLYN BRIDGE.

We now come to the saddest chapter of all, the one which records the melancholy end of one who, had he directed and devoted his life to the legitimate channel which God had so eminently fitted him, would have enjoyed the fruits of his labor, and his days would have been long in the land which his God had given him. His friends would not have been called upon to mourn his untimely fate, and no desperate deed on his part would have been necessary to retrieve his fallen fortunes. False friends accomplished his financial ruin ; false friends instilled into his enthusiastic mind the idea which resulted in his death.

That he could accomplish the deed in safety was not doubted for an instant by him. Had he not jumped from the tall mast-heads of ships ; had he not leaped in safety from the bridge at Occoquan ; from a ladder on the smoke-stack of a steamer, 110 feet, at Marshall Hall ; then why not leap from the Brooklyn bridge? He had evidently failed to remember that the malaria had crept into his system since then, contracted at Fortress Monroe, where the chills and fever find a safe harbor amid the rotting vegetation along the shores of Maryland and Virginia, and are wafted over to the Fortress, and find lodgment in the systems of the guests of the Hygeia Hotel. Calmly and coolly, we believe he could have performed the leap in safety two years ago.

In performing such a daring act it is but natural that some excitement should be felt. The Professor felt no fear. His first feat, which he accomplished successfully, was to elude the bridge police. This was no easy matter, and he had to use a subterfuge. This was attended with some excitement that produced nervousness, and, consequently, when he mounted the railing of the Brooklyn bridge he was a nervous man. He was physically unable to accomplish the feat, but the sports of New York had assembled to witness the performance, and amid them all, front and foremost on the tug chartered for the purpose, stood Boyton, of stuffed whale and

St. Jacob's Oil renown, his pretended friend, but really his arch enemy.

The Professor had been kept awake the whole night before, and was suffering from want of sleep and rest. He gazed down, far down upon the bosom of the East river, then upon the tug filled with his sporting friends; they had come out to witness the leap. He was no coward; no craven fear lurked in his heart; he would not disappoint them. Extending his right hand above his head, and turning his eyes toward Heaven, he stepped off into space; but the current of air was his unseen enemy, and the awful sequel is known.

The following account from the newspapers of New York and this city gives a connected narrative of his death-leap and interment:

To look at Professor Robert Emmet Odlum as he stood in a group of laughing friends yesterday morning, no one would have dreamed that he contemplated a jump from the Brooklyn bridge. His strong, dark features were lit up with smiles, and his brown eyes sparkled. He swung his large, sinewy hands about, and slapped his companions playfully, as he declared that he would make such a jump every morning before breakfast for exercise, if he were allowed. A very jolly fellow was this muscle-knotted, lithe teacher of swimming, who left his mother and sister in Washington a week ago to make the leap that had created so much talk. The Professor was entertaining a party of gentlemen at Captain Boyton's "Ship," in West Twenty-ninth street.

"Everybody says 'don't do it,'" he said, "and if I didn't the very same men would say I weakened. You can just bet all you have that I'm going to do this jump and come out all right."

Jere Dunn, Paddy Ryan, the fighter, and Muldoon, the wrestler, formed one group. Near by was a party of actors, including Henry E. Dixey, Eben Plympton and Harry Lacey; Cool Herbert, of St. Louis, and Major James Delehey chatted together. A few bets were made as to whether Odlum would make the jump or not.

Odlum donned a pair of gray trunks and a fancy red shirt, upon the bosom of which were worked his initials. Then he put on a pair of brown canvas shoes, a black, soft felt hat, and a blue jacket. Around his neck he tied a white silk handkerchief.

"I never felt better in my life," he said, "and I hope the police will not interfere and make me nervous when I jump. It is my business and not their's. God knows I wish it was over, for I'm nervous enough now. It isn't that I have any fears for the result, but I feel like an actor just before he goes on the stage in a new piece."

"Now," said Odlum, "if I should die I don't want the public to think that I had no good object in view. I want the *Herald* to explain that I have ·for years illustrated the fact that men do not die while falling through the air, and that, no matter if men or women were 100 feet high on· the roof of a burning building, they would not hesitate to jump into a net if they read that I had jumped 140 feet from the Brooklyn bridge."

There was great hilarity and story-telling during the next hour. Glasses clinked and bumpers were drank in honor of Odlum. He rubbed his hands and stroked his black mustache alternately. Then he smoked a few cigarettes. The people began to disappear in twos or threes. It was explained that a tug was waiting for the spectators at the barge office, and it was necessary to go down in small

11

parties in order not to excite the attention of the police, who were on the alert.

Odlum left the place at 4 o'clock, and went down town with two or three friends, including Mr. Cluss, son of Adolf Cluss, of Washington. He waited a few minutes in Ryan's, on Broadway, while a black covered wagon was procured near the post office. It was learned that a very large force of police was patrolling the carriageway of the bridge, and that unless some strategic measure was invented Odlum would be prevented from carrying out his purpose.

The Professor suddenly broke into a laugh as an idea struck him, and he explained that it would be a good thing to send a decoy on the bridge. James Haggart and Mr. Cluss got into a cab and drove on the south carriageway, followed by the wagon containing Odlum and a friend. The plan was for Mr. Haggart to pretend he was the jumper, and while the police were arresting him Odlum could make his leap.

When the two vehicles reached the bridge the cab was at once suspected. It was two hundred yards in front of the wagon in which the Professor sat. For hours the police had walked beside every cab that had crossed. One policeman held the head of the horse which pulled the cab. Another walked beside the cab and questioned Mr. Haggart, who said that he wanted to jump from the bridge and did not see why he should be interfered with. In a few moments the cab was surrounded by police as it continued toward Brooklyn at a very slow pace. Odlum clapped his hands and laughed.

"That's a joke on the police," he said, as he slipped off his outer clothing and sat in his shirt and trunks waiting for the critical moment. "They ain't smart enough to get on to us in here."

In the mean time the tug was crowded with spectators, and steamed up the East river to within a hundred yards of the bridge, where it lay in the stream.   As soon as the bridge police saw the vessel they knew that the time had come for the jump. Many of them got up on the carriage-way railing and peered down to see if there was any way by which Odlum could crawl out on the substructure of iron.   Thousands of people stopped on the promenade and the docks began to be crowded. Somehow or other everybody seemed to know what was coming and the greatest excitement prevailed. The jolly actors and sporting men on the tug laughed when they saw the police at their wits' end.   Sailors climbed up the masts of their vessels and waited for the fun.   Two or three sail and row boats put out from the shore, and a professional swimmer, hired by Mr. Odlum himself, appeared at the side of the tug in swimming tights ready to jump to the rescue.

Actor Dixey held a gold stop watch in his hand to time the jump, and around him pressed the merry party, cracking jokes and straining their eyes for a glimpse of Odlum.   Suddenly the wagon stopped and Odlum stepped out on the railing of the bridge with his face toward Governor's Island. Through the glasses every expression of his countenance could be seen.   He was very pale and looked down to see where the tug was.   Then he gave his trunks a hitch, threw his chest out and brought his feet close together.

He held his left arm rigidly down against his thigh and stretched his right hand at full length above his head with the palm open, his purpose being to use the right arm as a sort of rudder to maintain his equilibrium while shooting through the air.   Odlum was a perfect picture of manly grace and strength as he stood on the granite capping in the bright sunlight.

There was a dead silence as Odlum stepped off and shot downward. His head was pressed tightly against his uplifted arm and his eyes were turned upward. The jumper's chest was inflated until the muscles stood out in ridges and his heels were held together tightly. A strong wind was blowing, and as Odlum descended it seemed to turn him slightly around. For nearly a hundred feet he fell as straight as an arrow. Then he seemed to be conscious that he had lost his balance, and he made a rapid pass backward with his right hand. At the same moment his body assumed a slanting position in the air and he doubled up slightly. He struck the water with his feet and right hip. The force of the blow seemed to twist his body double, and as the plucky jumper disappeared a fountain of water twenty feet high was sent into the air.

"Three seconds and a half," said Actor Dixey, closing his watch.

A wild shout went up. It was a cry of fear and horror. Everybody knew that unless Odlum had struck the water with his body perpendicular he would be killed. For several moments no sign of the man could be discovered on the water. Then the red shirt was seen.

"He's dead," cried Jere Dunn. "This is horrible."

The swimmer in tights lost his head and did not know what to do. The people yelled at the top of their voices and everybody was wild with excitement. On the bow of the tug stood Captain Boyton watching for the reappearance of Odlum. The moment that he saw the red shirt the Captain peeled off his jacket and plunged into the river. He struck out powerfully, and in a few moments reached

Odlum, who was floating with his face downward and his red shirt torn in two by the force of the fall. Boyton raised the body upon his shoulders and swam against the tide with his heavy load toward a white ring life-preserver that had been thrown from the tug. He had to swim nearly fifty yards before he reached the small boat which had drifted against a mackerel schooner.

The murmur of the black thousands on the bridge and shores could be heard distinctly as the jumper's body, limp and helpless, was lifted into the boat. From there it was conveyed to the tug and laid upon blankets in the cook's galley. The back of the right hip was bruised and cut open by the water. All along the left side and back was a purple bruise. His eyes were shut and his muscles were as rigid as carved marble. Mr. Robertson and two other gentlemen assisted Captain Boyton in pouring brandy down the insensible man's throat, and rubbing it upon his head and breast. Paddy Ryan and Muldoon chafed his hands and arms. The actors and sports looked on with sad faces and watched for a sign of life. The face got whiter and the body darker. Then there was a feeble motion of the lips and Odlum was seen to gasp for breath. In a little while his chest heaved, and as he opened his big brown eyes there was a shout of joy. A terrible groan followed. Then Odlum passed one hand wearily across his face and caught wildly at the air. His friends called him by name. Then he smiled and moved his lips.

"Is it all over?" he murmured.

"Yes," answered Mr. Robertson.

"Did I make a good jump?"

"A fine one!"

"I'm so glad."

And Odlum turned upon his side. Then he seemed to get a sudden strength and pushed his attendants away. They called him endearing names, and begged him to speak. Finally a drop of bright blood leaked from his mouth.

"He's a dead man," whispered Muldoon.

The blood was wiped away and more followed it. Odlum noticed the stains upon the cloth used on his face and asked if he was spitting blood. Then he closed his eyes and his breathing became fainter and fainter. Once or twice he groaned deeply and said that his back pained him. The tug had steamed down the bay, and it was turned shoreward the moment that the crowd was satisfied that Odlum was dying. It reached Old Slip at ten minutes past 6 o'clock, thirty-five minutes after the jump was made. In a minute nearly all the party scrambled on shore and fled, leaving Captain Boyton and several friends with the dying man. Muldoon notified the police, who sent for an ambulance. It was twenty minutes before the ambulance arrived, and just as it rattled on the dock Odlum ceased breathing, and his strong arms were folded upon his breast.

Surgeon Hathaway examined the body and declared that no bones were broken. He said that some of Odlum's internal organs had been burst by the shock of the fall. Detective Hagan appeared on the dock and placed all the reporters and other people on the tug under arrest until a squad of policemen arrived and escorted them to the Old Slip station house, where their names were entered as witnesses for the coroner's inquest.

The corpse remained on the dock in charge of a policeman, surrounded by hundreds of people, until Coroner Kennedy removed it. It was learned that James Haggart, who decoyed the police after his cab, in order to give Odlum a clear path, was arrested and locked up in Brooklyn. It appears that, in order to more completely sell the public, Mr. Haggart pretended that he was trying to undress himself. The charge against him is that of disorderly conduct.—*New York Herald.*

ARRIVAL OF THE BODY IN WASHINGTON.

The remains of Robert E. Odlum, who was killed Tuesday evening by jumping from the Brooklyn bridge into the river below, arrived here this morning at 8:05 o'clock, having left New York at midnight. The remains were inclosed in a handsome mahogany casket, with silver handles and trimmings. The plate and inscription will be supplied by relatives and friends. The body was attired in a full dress suit of black.

Mr. Herbert said to a reporter that no one deplored the result more than Captain Boyton, who had done all he could to dissuade Odlum from his purpose. Odlum said that he was certain he could do it, and argued that he would be in the air but two and a half seconds, and by falling with one arm close to the side and the other extended above his head he would strike the water feet first and do it. They were quite certain, he said, that when Odlum went on the bridge to make the leap he would be stopped.

The funeral will take place at 4 o'clock tomorrow.

Mr. C. S. Moore and other friends, with Mr. J. C. Lee, met the body at the depot.

The remains were at first removed to Mr. Lee's undertaking establishment, and then taken to his residence, 504 Thirteenth street, northwest. The funeral arrangements have been taken in hand by

Messrs. C. S. Moore, William Dickson and Frank K. Ward.

Many of Odlum's friends viewed the remains to-day. The face has good color, and a most natural and placid expression. His friends express some indignation at the efforts of Captain Boyton and others, who were with Odlum in New York, to make it appear that they were bending every energy to prevent Odlum from making the leap. The fact that some one paid all the expenses of carriages and a tug, and went to the trouble of very elaborate preparations, they think establishes the fact that Odlum was rather encouraged than otherwise in his rash undertaking.

The autopsy took place in New York yesterday afternoon. The spleen, liver and kidneys were found to be badly ruptured from the shock in striking the water. There was a deposit of tuberculosis at the base of the left lung ; the right kidney was full of cystic cavities, and the left lung gave evidences of slight fatty degeneration. The first, third and fifth ribs were found to be broken. The doctors say that death was due to concussion. The marks on the body were similar to those found on the bodies of men who have been crushed by the caving in of the earth.—*Star, May* 21.

After the departments closed yesterday afternoon the residence where the remains of the dead athlete, Odlum, lay was thronged with callers to see the body, who continued arriving until quite late at night. Probably no one person in private life here possessed so large a circle of personal friends and acquaintances, for "Bob" Odlum, as they affectionately knew him, was a man of such kind-hearted ways that he drew friends to him without effort on his part. It was noticeable that large numbers were attracted there, however, only through an idle, morbid curiosity, and of these, to their shame, a large proportion were females.

At the funeral at 4 o'clock this afternoon the pall-bearers will be Messrs. William Dickson, Frank K. Ward, Washington Nailor, Jacob A. Rudd, Robert M. Vanneman and Edward D. Wright. All of the funeral arrangements have been under the direction of Mr. Charles S. Moore, who remained at the house last night beside the body.

Early last evening Mrs. Odlum, the aged mother of the dead man, and his sister, Mrs. Charlotte Smith, with the latter's son, arrived, where they remained during the night in an upper room. Both remained for a while beside the remains, repeating the Catholic prayers for the dead. The grief of Mrs. Odlum and her daughter was so violently expressed in plaintive cries that it was deemed best to urge their removal up stairs, where it was far on into the night before either became sufficiently calmed to control their feelings. The scene was a deeply painful one to witness.

As early as 8 o'clock this morning the stream of callers began again, many of poor "Bob's" most intimate friends returning again and again to the coffin's side.—*Critic, May* 22.

The funeral of the late Robert E. Odlum took place yesterday afternoon from No. 504 Thirteenth street, northwest. The body lay in one of the parlors, where the funeral services were held, surrounded by numerous floral designs, a great beauty conspicuous among these being a fac-simile of the Brooklyn bridge, which was donated by the Light Infantry Corps. The house was crowded with the friends of the deceased, who listened attentively while Father Ahern, of St. Matthew's church, pronounced a glowing tribute to the dead athlete. The notoriety which the deceased's last exploit gained him attracted many from idle curiosity, and a crowd of about six hundred people gathered in the street and waited to see the cortege start for the cemetery.—*Post, May* 23.

Rev. Father Ahern, of St Matthew's church, performed the Catholic burial service and made a very touching and eloquent address. After speaking of the brevity of life and the certainty of death, and the knowledge men possessed of hastening to this critical period as fast as the wings of time could carry them, and the impossibility of any one ever retracing his steps after having entered the bounds of eternity, he drew a lesson of the necessity of being ever prepared to meet death. In reference to Odlum's moral responsibility for his own death, he said: "What the world may think of the responsibility of the man who expected to leap from the balustrade of the Brooklyn bridge, and by some act of sagacity to elude the effect of the accelerating power of gravity, ought certainly to be no more condemnatory than its judgment of a person who, believing that God has established an order of sequence in morals, yet expects to violate with impunity the moral law of his Creator. The moral laws of God can no more be varied than physical law. The results which God has connected with actions will ineviably occur. And yet we see men enjoying the esteem of communities, and who are habitually violating the moral law, yet expecting to escape the consequences which God has established. The only difference is in the order of sequence that the violation of physical law is attended with immediate results, while in morals it is often long delayed. And, therefore, the Scripture

tells us that because sentence is not executed speedily against an evil act the hearts of the sons of men
are fully set to do evil. The consequences which
society has connected with the act of this man ought
to have determined him not to undertake it. To us
it seems a rash act—a reckless act, a foolhardy act,
a hazardous attempt, endangering human life. Its
result, indeed, proved fatal; but let the result of
an action be what it may, we hold the man responsible solely on the ground of intention, and
Robert Odlum was a voluntary, intelligent man,
capable of foreseeing the result of an exertion of
his power, with that exertion subject to his own
free will. We do not know what the motive of
the man was, but we deem it to have been a better
one than that of merely securing the vain applause
of a wonder-loving world. In his own mind he was
justified, not merely hoping that he would perform
this feat successfully, but in the firm conviction
that he would accomplish it easily. A professional
athlete, he had often performed similar feats of
daring, and his conscience rendered satisfactory
testimony of his ability to repeat them. Regarding himself as a distinct and accountable individual,
to whom God had given wonderful physical strength
as a means of happiness, he recognized the right to
exert the powers of his body as he willed. Unconscious of danger himself, he did not think he
was committing an overt act against society, and
the proof of forfeiture to the claims of society rests
with those who would now exclude him, while they
would have, perhaps, most loudly applauded and
praised him had he accomplished his daring feat
successfully.''

Father Ahern referred to Odlum's generous
character and manly conduct in having many times

risked his life to save the lives of others who were perishing in the water.

The remains were followed by a long line of carriages to Mt. Olivet cemetery, where they were placed in the vault.—*Star, May* 23.

The feat which Mr. Odlum attempted, and which resulted in his death, had been a subject of conversation with him for some time past, and he had even made a plan of the bridge to facilitate his movements in making the jump. It was not thought here that he would do it, and it is believed that he never would have attempted it had he not been urged by Capt. Paul Boyton, who telegraphed him on several occasions an invitation to come to New York. To his landlady Odlum talked quite freely on the subject, and informed her of the advances made by Boyton to him, in which the latter told him to make his place in New York a home and to come on and take in the situation thoroughly before making the attempt. The newspaper notoriety which the affair had gained for him, it is thought, had also considerable influence with him. "I will not undertake the thing," he said, unless there is money in it. In that case I will risk it." He said that he expected a telegram from Boyton, which would decide the matter. On Wednesday the expected dispatch arrived, and Odlum prepared to start for New York the same night. It was noticed that he became unusually thoughtful and quiet, as though he had some presentiment of the tragic culmination to which the affair was destined. When night arrived he suddenly changed his mind and decided not to start until morning. When taking leave of his landlady she said, with a doubtful shake of her head, "Mr. Odlum, I hope it will end all right."

" Don't talk like that," he exclaimed, quite dis-
concerted, but almost immediately regained his
composure. He took leave of only a few friends
and left without intimating his intentions to his
mother. Her first knowledge was gained from the
New York *Sun*, and she immediately telegraphed
to the New York authorities to prevent the attempt
under any circumstances. No further news, with
the exception of a few rumors, was received from
him until last night, when the following dispatch from Captain Boyton arrived at Willard's
Hotel :

"Robert E. Odlum jumped off Brooklyn bridge
this morning and was killed. Body recovered.
Please notify relatives what disposition to be made
of body."

When his mother was informed of the circumstance she was nearly prostrated with grief, and
declared openly that Boyton was the cause of his
death. The same feeling prevailed among Odlum's
friends, and they all concurred in condemning the
share Boyton had taken in the matter. It was
stated that Boyton's anxiety was caused by his
having staked $1,000 that Odlum would make the
jump.

The mother and sister of Mr. Odlum reside on
Four-and a-half street between C street and Penn-
sylvania avenue. The latter relative became almost
uncontrollable with grief and excitement on learning at police headquarters that the report was true.
—*Post*, *May* 25.

No ; poor " Bob" Odlum was not a "fool" nor
a "crank," but a brave, honest, kindly-hearted
man, who desired fame or notoriety for a legitimate purpose—that it might help him in his business. He had reason to believe that he could

safely perform the feat which cost his life, for he had dared other feats almost as dangerous. Led on step by step by the fascination of aquatic exploits, he met his death. He had saved many other lives, his own he could not save. He deserves no sneers.—*National Republican*.

The *Hatchet* readers know the fearful fate of that strong swimmer and brave, generous man, Robert Emmet Odlum. They have read the details of his perilous plunge from the Brooklyn bridge into the cruel waters one hundred and forty feet below. They know the fatal result. It is unnecessary to go into the sad details again.

As Father Ahern said at the funeral on Friday, "what we hold a man to are his intentions." Thus judged, our dead friend's memory stands before a world ever readier to censure than to praise, honorably vindicated from the flippant charge of foolhardiness and a mere seeking after notoriety. He believed that he could make the daring leap successfully, and so believing he felt it his duty, not only to himself and to those dependent upon him, but to the world, to challenge fate.

In a conversation with the writer a few nights preceding his going to New York, Mr. Odlum explained a theory he had long held, that every fire company should be provided with strong nettings which could be immediately stretched and into which the unfortunates beleaguered by fire and smoke, sinking floors and falling walls, could jump without peril to life or limb. He argued that most people were afraid to jump from a high place, even when threatened with a fiery death, because of an absurd idea that they would die in the air. By making his leap from the Brooklyn bridge he hoped forever to dispel this fallacy, and open the way to the introduction of his netting idea in fire departments. His plan appeared to us feasible, and his untimely death while engaged in an experiment looking partly toward its development and application, makes him a martyr to humanity of the same class, if not the same degree, as the physician or nurse who falls a victim while extending succor to the plague-stricken.

The funeral took place on Friday afternoon, and was largely attended by the deceased's friends. There were numerous floral offerings, the chief one being a representation of the Brooklyn bridge, sent by his comrades of the Light Infantry. Father Ahern pronounced an appropriate and touching discourse, and all that was mortal of one of the truest-hearted and most manly of men was consigned to Mt. Olivet cemetery.—*The Hatchet, May* 24.

One of the saddest features in regard to Odlum's death is that the man was wasted. He had occasionally jumped from various heights into the water, but his jumps were unostentatious and the public was never made to suffer from them. There was really no reason why the man should not have lived for many years and no one have been the worse for it.

Odlum is dead, but Boyton and many other well-known persons are still painfully alive. There was every reason why Boyton should have jumped from the bridge. For the last ten years the public has endured his advertising voyages in his rubber suit, and he has never failed to outrage public decency by arriving safely at his destination. Had he decided to jump from the bridge there is not a man in this city who would have been so heartless as to interfere with him. The very policemen would have forgotten their orders and would have turned their backs on Boyton as soon as he made his appearance on the bridge. Indeed, it would have been easy to raise by popular subscription a large sum of money to induce Boyton to jump.

But Mr. Boyton, instead of satisfying the longings of his fellow-citizens, has never dreamed of jumping from the bridge. Several other men, every one of whom was in every way adapted to jump off the bridge, imitated Boyton's example and helped Odlum to throw himself away. We naturally feel sorry that Odlum was wasted, but our sorrow that these men did not jump in his place is necessarily greater.—*New York Times.*

A REVIEW OF THE MANY COMMENTS OF THE PRESS
ON THE TRAGEDY.

What notoriety was given the tragedy of the Brooklyn bridge is due to the great dailies of New York city, notably the *Herald.* Why will leading newspapers devote four or five columns to such tragedies? Why did leading newspapers, like the *Sun* and *Herald,* send their sporting specials days before the occurrence to interview Professor Odlum, to walk the bridge in his company, as did Mr. Henry Creelman, of the New York *Herald?* He informed me himself that he accompanied my son on the Sunday previous to the jump, and was in his company *constantly* Why did the editor of the New York *Sun* refuse to give the name of his sporting special when I called on him? Had that special committed a crime? What was there to evade? I afterward discovered his name was Amos Cummings. Why did Mr. Creelman say that some of the first and best gentlemen of New York, among them Mr. Chamberlain, James Gordon Bennett's private secretary, witnessed the jump? Why did the proprietor of the *Herald* send his private secretary to witness the jump? Did they know the jump would take place? Yes! Did they take any step to prevent it? No! but encouraged it by their presence. Under the laws of the State of New York, are they innocent of any participation in the death of Robert Emmet Odlum? Knowing positively that the leap would be made, the hour appointed for the same, did they inform the police? No! Well, then, if any crime has been committed they are aiders and abettors, and are partly responsible for the death of the unfortunate man. Tom Murphy, son of the ex-collector of the port of New York, and fifty other "select sports," made bets as to the result. They "aided, abetted and encouraged Robert Emmet Odlum to commit an act imminently dangerous to human life," and stand convicted by their own testimony out of their own mouths.

All this is cruel enough, but the most poignant, unkind cuts of all are the comments of the same press after the spirit of the unfortunate young man had taken its flight from earth. If they were participants, which they were, they should "say nothing but good of the dead." No light remarks, no jeers should be tolerated in a press that encouraged the deed, "the deep damnation of his taking off." Editorials condemning the act after it had been committed comes with bad grace from these journals. Editorials written before the act to prevent the catastrophe might have prevented it. Editorials afterward are out of place, ill-timed and serve no purpose but to wound the heart of his aged and afflicted mother, already bowed down with a weight of woe the grave only can lift.

"Charity covereth a multitude of sins," and charity should have dictated every editorial emanating from the press of New York when commenting on the tragedy of the Brooklyn bridge.

12

CHAPTER XI.

LETTERS.

The Boyton Letters--an Explanation to the Public.

The following reasons are given to the public for publishing the letters of Captain Boyton to my son : It was natural, under all the circumstances, for me to attach the blame of his death to Paul Boyton. To my certain knowledge during the last few years Robert was the recipient of many letters from him, together with telegrams, urging him to make the perilous leap. "If you don't, somebody else will," and the enthusiastic young man waited for no more. He went on to New York, and the sequel is known to the reader.

After the tragedy Captain Boyton read some comments in the New York *News* and other papers showing the public feeling against him, and charging him with being accessory to my poor boy's fate. A few days thereafter I received a long and penitent letter from Boyton, which reads as follows :

NEW YORK, *May* 27, 1885.

Mrs. ODLUM.

DEAR MADAM : Yesterday I shipped per Adams Express the effects left at my house by your son Robert. Dear Mrs. Odlum, it is with feelings of great hesitation that I address you after all the hatred and cruel things you have said about me, and yet I consider it my duty to write to you. The great God, who knows all, knows that I did every thing in my power to prevent the jump, and the same God knows that I am not his murderer you accuse me of being. You cannot imagine with

what grief and sorrow I read your accusation. I
was in bed at the time, ill with a heavy cold, and
it almost broke my heart to have you think that I
was in any way responsible for the death of a friend
whom I loved for his good nature and brave heart.
I have one thing to say that I am sure will give
you consolation.   On that fatal Thursday morning
Robert got up early and disappeared for four hours.
I did not know where he had gone, and hoped he
had taken my advice and left New York.   Since
then I have discovered that he went from my house
to the Church of the Redemptorist Fathers, where
a friend of mine saw him go to the confessional
and receive holy communion.   I thank the Lord.
May God rest the soul of poor, poor Rob.   Mrs.
Odlum, I wish I could go to you, and, kneeling at
your feet, tell you all I did to turn him away from
his determination, and to convince you that I am
not his murderer in deed or thought.   I would not
have gone to the river to witness his leap but for
the thought that I might be of assistance to him.
In answer to my entreaties that he should abandon
his idea, he said: "This feat will give me fame
and a reputation that will survive me, plenty of
engagements, and thus enable me to help my mother
and myself, as I would wish to do and as I have
not been able to do for a couple of years.   Don't
try and turn me from the only chance I see left to
make a name and a fortune."

Poor, brave, gentle-hearted Bob—I am sure he
thought of you in his last moments.   I too have a
mother, who has read all about your son's sad fate
and your accusation has cut her to the heart.   She
has just written to me saying she would pray every
day for the poor boy as long as she lived.   My wife
is doing the same and will continue to do so.   She
knows that you are mistaken, for she heard me im-

ploring Bob to abandon the idea. She and I pray
for him every night, and as long as we have a dollar to spare it will be spent in masses for the re-
pose of his soul. If you think I am guilty of luring
on your son to his death I simply bare my head and
accept it as a punishment for many a sin I have
committed, but God knows of this one I am innocent. God bless, comfort, and console you, dear
Mrs. Odlum.

Yours sincerely and sorrowfully,
PAUL BOYTON.

His letter was so contrite and humble in its tone,
and affected so much genuine sorrow that I felt
almost inclined to forgive him for whatever part
he had taken in the transaction. This letter was
published in all the great dailies of the country,
and spread by himself broadcast, and after seeing
which, I concluded to visit New York to see if my
son had left some word or message for his afflicted
mother. I was confident of being well received by
Boyton. I wished to visit New York for another
purpose, viz., to learn all I could concerning the
details of the affair, and to recover important papers
and letters from persons in New York urging him
to the act, as these were missing when his trunk
and clothes were returned.

I arrived at the Astor House about midnight,
but the hotel being full, the clerk very kindly sent
a porter with me to the International Hotel, where
I was courteously received and kindly treated.
After the reception of Captain Boyton's letter, I
concluded I would call to see him, which I did the
day after my arrival at his "Ship." I reached
his place about 10 o'clock a. m., and was told by
a man, who claimed to be his manager, that the
captain was still in bed, having been up the night

previous very late. After Boyton was informed
of my presence in his saloon he sent me word down
stairs by his manager and Cool Herbert that he
would call at my hotel to see me. I expressed my
astonishment to Herbert that he should have repre-
sented through the press that he was a great friend
of my family, when the truth was I had never seen
him but once, when he came on with my son's body,
and by his loud boasting of what expenses he had
incurred and the trouble he had been subjected to
excited the disgust of his auditory. I told him I
wished to say nothing to him, that I came to see
Captain Boyton.

I returned to my hotel, but Captain Boyton never
came ; but two men did come, styling themselves
the lawyer and the judge, and representing themselves in the interest of Captain Boyton. They
were manufactured for the occasion, and but for
my recent sad affliction I should have been highly
amused at their attempt to intimidate me. They
first endeavored to impress me with the belief that
it was my duty to keep silence, while they went
through the comedy which they had committed
to memory.

"Madam," said one, "I am the judge and my
friend here is the lawyer, and we have all the
papers in this case." Here the judge held up a
large bundle of papers, and continued, addressing
me. "It is absolutely necessary, madam, for you
to keep silent ; you must not even see or say anything to any reporter who may call upon you for
an interview. Captain Boyton is under a rent of
$5,000 annually, and you must be careful not to
say anything which might injure his business.
The laws of New York are very severe on this
subject, and inflict severe penalties against any
one who speaks ill of another. Here is the law and

here are all the papers. Isn't this so, brother lawyer?'' And the lawyer would bow and humbly answer, "Yes."

"There was no one to blame, madam, but your son,'' said the lawyer. Isn't this so, Mr. Judge?'' And the judge would embrace his bundle of papers, and boldly answer: "Nobody else to blame.'' They both kept this up for some time, telling me of the severe punishments in store for me unless I kept my lips closed in regard to Boyton. I was too angry and in too much distress to notice the affair in its proper light at the time, but have since been impressed with the ridiculous rascality of the whole affair. I now distinctly remember having seen my judge at Paul Boyton's in the morning when I called there. He was coming down stairs with Cool Herbert, and the judicial ermine was conferred upon the fellow to try my case—convict me and acquit Boyton.

Perhaps this man is known as the "Ship's attorney,'' to try special cases in which Boyton is party defendant. Mr. Judge and Mr. Lawyer left me firmly impressed that I was frightened. They advised me to keep quiet and leave the city at once, as the laws of New York were very strict, and they should be grieved to see me in trouble.

I can imagine what the public will say say when they read this statement. It is literally true, and gives a picture of the characters of the crew of the "Ship'' commanded by Captain Paul Boyton.

I make the following extracts from Paul Boyton's letters and telegrams:

BALTIMORE, 15-6-'80.
No more, dear Bob. I will never forget your kindness to me, and I thank you from the bottom

of my heart. When I get off the rocks and well to windward, you may rest assured I will prove to you that I am not ungrateful.

Your sincere friend,   PAUL.

—

BALTO., MD., *June* 4, 1880.

PROF. R. ODLUM: If you can get Corcoran, telegraph Baltimore *Sun* job printing department to go ahead with Boyton bills. No time to lose.

PAUL.

Here is a sample of brag and bluster:

PROVIDENCE, R. I., 26, 7, '80.

MY DEAR AND KIND FRIEND BOB: Enclosed find $25 to pay the *Republican*. I am ashamed of myself for not sending it before. Tell me how much more is still owing and I will remit. I received your kind letter, but I have been so busy that it was impossible to answer it. I will do so in a few days when I have a few moments to spare. I wish you were with me now; plenty of business. I will see you this fall, as I will be in Baltimore. I am matched to swim Fearn, champion of England, Aug. 17th, for $1,000. I often think of you, and I will never forget your kindness. Dear Bob, you must excuse these few lines, as I must run for the train. Address Worcester, Mass. Remember me to all the old friends.

With a grateful heart, I remain your sincere friend,   PAUL BOYTON.

Tell me the amount now due in your next.

BOYTON IN LUCK.

ON BOARD THE FIERY AND UNTAMED STEAMER "ARKANSAS," MISSISSIPPI, 26, 5, '81.

MY DEAR BOB: Well, what must you think of me? Don't blame me until I tell you a few lies to excuse myself. I am at present bound up to St. Paul, from where I will commence a voyage of 1,000 down to Cairo. I think it will take me fully 20 days to make the run, as the current is very sluggish; but the river is a beauty. How I do wish you were along; we could just have the gayest kind of a time. What a "head" I had on me the morning I parted with you. It reminded me of the old days of the "moral show." I have an angel at present in the shape of a manager who "puts up" for everything. I am going to "use" him.

Ten thousand thanks, dear Bob, for your kindness to me during my last visit. I assure you I am truly grateful. Don't fail to write me.

Ever your friend,   PAUL.

The following letter from Boyton we give entire; it is dated—

FLUSHING 10, 4, '82.

DEAR BOB: Your letter of the 5th came to hand this a. m. I got home about a month ago, with a fine collection of malaria, picked up on the Missouri, Arkansas and Yazoo rivers, in my skin. I had a pretty tough time with the fever and chills, but I am about through with it now. I resigned my position in the house of Vogeler & Co. on the 9th of last month, so at present I am looking around for a good thing. Fred. J. Engelhardt wants me to go in with him on his big whale. He made me a very liberal offer of one-third interest in the show, and it is now doing well in Atlanta, Ga. This week will decide whether I join him or not. Vogeler was anxious to have me go to Europe for him, but I have found out that working for a salary *don't* pay. I came out of his employ in debt to him. You have to spend too much money on newspaper men, and that must be done out of your own pocket. I was thinking that in managing the whale and working my own "moral show" in whenever a chance offered, I could do pretty well with Fred. Engelhardt. In regard to going to California, I cannot see a chance to do so at present. By the way, I had a letter from Daily, the champion swimmer of California, a few days ago, asking me to come out, as he intends to get up a lot of aquatic fetes there this summer. There might be something in it. I cannot go, as I have not money enough to move myself and properties out so far. The man to work a jump from the East River bridge is Richard K. Fox; write him. I will see him again and will speak to him about it. With my usual luck I am "on the rocks," but I hope for a change soon. I wish to God a good war would start up to give poor devils like me a chance.

With the kindest regards of your old and sincere friend,   PAUL.

Address Flushing, L. I., N. Y.

It will be observed by the reader that Professor Odlum is referred by Boyton to Richard K. Fox, to make the preliminaries for a jump from the Brooklyn bridge, and promised to see Fox on the subject. Does this look like an attempt to prevent the jump on Boyton's part? Is it not rather an encouraging message to arrange preliminaries? If I know a man intends committing a desperate deed, and I do not take steps to prevent it, am I not guilty of aiding in the transaction? This is common sense and admits of no argument.

There are upward of fifty other letters relating to St. Jacob's Oil, "the stuffed whale," and the wild projects of Boyton, in every one of which he requests Professor Odlum to become a participant. His "My dear Bob" generally had to pay all the bills and assume all the pecuniary responsibilities, such as chartering steamers, getting bills and posters printed, &c. His letters breathe a spirit of bombast, low cunning, and we will not inflict our readers with a perusal. They will be shown any one desiring to see them.

HE SURRENDERS THE WHALE.

ROCHESTER, N. Y., 14, 7, '82.

MY DEAR BOB: Your kind letter of June 21st came duly to hand. I would have answered it long before this, but I have been so upset and busy that I assure you I had no time. I parted company with the infernal old whale at Harrisburgh, and I am only sorry I did not do so long before I did. Since then (two weeks) I have been running my own "moral show" to a big business. This is a new country up here for me, and I have succeeded in making a big hit.

With kindest regards, dear Bob, your sincere friend, PAUL.

THE CAPTAIN WISHES THE PROFESSOR TO FIND AN ANGEL.

WASHINGTON HEIGHTS, N. Y. C., 23d, '84.

MY DEAR BOB: I presume you could not make any arrangements with the exhibition people. Well, it is just as good, as I fear I would be unable to go. I have an idea that I think you might work out. If you can get some *angel* to *put up* I can furnish you with a dress and full suit of properties, some splendid three-sheet pictorials and descriptive posters, window bills, blocks, &c.—*a whole moral show complete*—and the use of my name.

You could take in New Orleans, and then take a trip through Texas, a State I have never been in; also the Red River country, which would pay well. Then you could run across to California—it would be new there. You can work all those places this winter if you can only find an angel to put up the *dust*. See if you can work it. Merry Christmas.
          Your friend,   PAUL.

—

BALTIMORE, MD., *May* 26, 1884.
To ROBERT ODLUM,
          Natatorium, Washington, D. C.
Take the Corcoran and commence advertising. Will write all particulars.
          PAUL BOYTON.

—

WASHINGTON HEIGHTS,
NEW YORK CITY, 17–11–'84.
MY DEAR BOB: I would have been off to China in September, and if I had closed the contract you would have been included in it, as I had you in "my mind's eye." They wanted me to go, but I could not make up my mind to leave my wife alone so soon after marriage. I was not very successful this summer. I did not work much anyhow, as I was not well. I am expecting to go into business soon with the assistance of my father-in-law. At present I am doing nothing. How are things in Washington? Drop me a line once in a while.
          With kind regards, your friend,
          PAUL.

—

NEW YORK, *Dec.* 14, '84.
Prof. R. ODLUM.
MY DEAR SIR: Captain Boyton told me yesterday that he had heard from you. It might be fixed that you and I might work business. You will,

perhaps, recollect meeting me when I was with the captain in Washington with the whale. I have been his manager for years. Let me know as quick as you can what is your purpose.

Very truly yours,

SAM C. FREEMAN,
St. Omer Hotel, 6th ave. and 23d st.

These letters go to show that, since the year 1880, Paul Boyton has used the skill of Professor Odlum for his own aggrandisement—for the purpose of making money. When his fortune was on the wane, and he found himself "on the rocks," to use his favorite expression, he would always call on his "My Dear Bob" to help him out of his financial straits. It was always contended by the friends of Professor Odlum that Paul Boyton first suggested the idea of his jumping from the Brooklyn bridge. A word to the police from Boyton would have prevented the leap, if he was so opposed to it, as he would have the relations of Professor Odlum believe. Instead of taking this step, a tug was chartered, filled with the sporting element of New York, and anchored in the East river near the bridge. The reporters of all the great dailies of New York were among the crowd while the brave but unfortunate Professor had to resort to a subterfuge to escape the vigilance of the bridge police. Paul Boyton eagerly watched and waited for the coming of the Professor, and when the intrepid Odlum escaped from the wagon and mounted the railing amid the horrified pedestrians on the bridge, Paul Boyton was prepared with his life preservers to rescue him in case of accident, but had taken no step to prevent the fatal leap. The public asks, "Was Paul Boyton an accessory to the death of Robert Emmet Odlum?" and the

evidence and facts of the case plainly answer,
" Yes." His relatives will view him in that light,
and the reason that posterity will give for his
criminality in this sad tragedy will be that he
was "on the rocks," and the reckless daring of
Professor Odlum was the hopeful means of setting
him afloat. That thousands of dollars changed
hands on the occasion is a known fact—while a
diligent search after the sad catastrophe revealed
the fact—that *ninety cents* was all that honored
the treasury of Professor Odlum. It was a grand
tragedy—a matter of speculation in which the
sports of New York were the winners. Their ill-
gotten gains were obtained at the price of the life
of Professor Odlum, who, like the story of Damon
and Pythias, surrendered all—even his life—for
the benefit of so-called friends.

These miserable sports may have their day, but
the day of retribution will come when a just God will
call them to account for speculating in the blood of a
fellow-man, whose enthusiasm overcame his discretion. Paul Boyton and the sports have a fearful
deed to answer for. Vengeance is mine, saith the
Lord, and to his judgment we submit the affair with
all its horrid details. Their treatment to the mother
of the deceased, when she went on to see if her boy had
not left some message or letter for her, proves their
heartlessness and their guilt. Their desire to hush
up the affair, their seeming want of knowledge of
the details, the mysterious disappearance of the
fund said to have been contributed for her relief,
shows that with the burial of the body of their victim
they wished to wash their hands of the matter, and
let the memory of the man they had coaxed and
cajoled and invited to death sleep in oblivion, to
be mentioned and cared for by them no more. Such
is Paul Boyton and such are the sports of New

York. The true friends of the unfortunate Professor hear their names with detestation, and regret that it requires men of such evil propensity to form a world.

The attention of the press of the country is called to the conduct of Boyton in this sad affair. After the publication of this chapter he will be known as a miserable pretender, an advertising agent. He would have the world believe that he is a prodigy of valor, possessing some great art to astonish the world by his daring feats. In unmasking this hypocrite the world will thank the author of this book. The letters from him which are now published will do that effectually. His pretended friendship for Professor Odlum was a sham—put on to fill his purse. There is nothing genuine about the man. Like his "stuffed whale," he is large to look upon but very small intrinsically. He loves to discourse on sharks and other monsters of the deep, seemingly unconscious that he is himself a man-shark with jaws extended to swallow up the life, the fame, the winnings of his fellow-man. If you will take the trouble to investigate you will find that the loudest blast to Boyton's fame is blown from his own fog-horn. An artful advertising dodger, he is careful on all occasions to advertise himself, to show his natural propensity to yarn and imitate Gulliver or the Baron Munchausen. We reproduce an account of himself, given by himself, of his wonderful adventures in Peru. It is taken from the Washington *Post* of May, 1881 :

PAUL BOYTON IN PERU.

Terrible Scenes at Chorillos—Minister Christiancy's Lively Race for Life at the Battle of Miraflores.

Captain Paul Boyton made a flying visit to

Washington yesterday, passing a few hours with his aquatic friend, Professor Odlum, and leaving on the owl train for his home at Flushing, Long Island. A *Post* representative came across him at the Natatorium, sporting with the lads in the big bath-tub, and evidently as happy as a clam. After he had left the water and dried himself, he gave a favorable response to the reporter's demand for breezy information.

"I've been down in South America helping the Peruvians fight their enemies," said the intrepid swimmer, bronzed and swarthy, "and I am glad that I got out with a whole skin to my back. I tell you it was perfect h—l down there. In a few days, as soon as I am rested, I intend to swim from the head of the Mississippi to St. Louis, a distance of 1,200 miles. Then I will finish my book, 'Roughing it in Rubber, or 10,000 Miles in a Life-Saving Dress.' I expect to make money enough out of the book to live like a lord for the rest of my days."

"Let's get out of the water and talk about terrestrial affairs. How did they treat you in Peru?"

"I went into the Peruvian service last fall, in the torpedo squadron. I sailed under the assumed name of Paul Delaport. Had I been allowed to carry my plans into execution, I think I could have destroyed the Chilian fleet, with 10,000 troops aboard, that landed the invading army on Peruvian soil. I sunk my torpedo boat to escape capture, and then joined the Peruvian land forces defending Chorillos. The enemy, with bombs and shells, drove us out and we retreated to Miraflores. The enemy acted brutally at Chorillos; they butchered thousands of men, women and children in cold blood. The Peruvian Indians were just as blood-thirsty. I saw one of them murder a young

German, a wounded prisoner, who fought with the Chilians ; he was a nephew, I am told, of General Von Moltke, the great general."

" Were the Peruvians game birds? "

" Not over game, and some of them cowards. The battle of Miraflores was the hottest kind of a fight. The air was filled with bullets as with a swarm of flies. The foreign ministers were scared almost to death. I saw Minister Christiancy running under full sails across the fields toward Lima. He was in his shirt-sleeves. It was a go-as-you-please race for life. The Peruvians were utterly routed. Even the mules, with the ammunition in sacks on their backs, stampeded, and the powder for the fighters ran short. All steered for Lima. There murder and rapine reigned with bloody hands. I was placed at the head of a company of Americans, and, with other foreigners, fought for order. The negroes were the most savage portion of the mob. The poor Chinamen were indiscriminately butchered and robbed."

" Do you have any hope for Peru, now under the heels of her conquerors? "

" It is hard to say. Pierola, the dictator, is a brave and good man, and an excellent general. With a few good men-of-war he could, I think, restore the republic. Let the Chilian fleet be destroyed and the Peruvians would soon annihilate their invaders."

" How were affairs in Lima when you left? "

" Words cannot paint the horrors. The Chilians are in occupation and they are brutal. It was a common sight to see a squad of Chilian soldiers wheel out of the barracks, followed by a few wretched, hollow-eyed Peruvians, bare-headed and in chains, priests in their robes beside them, holding up the crucifix and offering consolation. At

the first public square they would halt, fasten the
poor devils to posts or trees, and shoot them down
like dogs. Even courts-martial were ignored. I
have seen the Chilian soldiers tie up the poor
Peruvians in the main streets and flog them until
their backs were covered with blood. The women,
thank God, were not molested ; they are very
pretty, and braver than the men. They intensely
hate the invaders, but generally keep in doors.
As I left Lima I saw a frightful, horrible scene.
On the battle-field of Miraflores there were many
dead—5,000 Chilians and 3,500 Peruvians. The
vanquished had fled ; the victors were too intent
on plunder and rapine to turn grave-diggers. The
corpses were swollen into enormous proportions
under the tropical sun, and emitted the foulest
odors. Something had to be done ; so the Chilians
hired a lot of Chinamen to burn the bodies. The
heathens would punch holes in each dead body,
pour in coal oil and then apply fire. As I passed
by the battle-field at night, a blue flame issued
out of each corpse, giving a still ghastlier hue to
the swollen and distorted faces of the dead. The
horrid sight will be with me to my dying hour."

While Boyton was in Peru performing these
wonderful feats, Professor Odlum happened to
have a friend in Peru from whom he received
letters. From one under date of Matucana, April
14, 1881, the statement of this correspondent and
that of Boyton differ so widely about the valor displayed by the captain that we publish it entire:

MATUCANA, *April 14th*, 1881.
MY DEAR FRIEND : How do you do, and how in
blazes are you getting on ? I suppose you will be
surprised to hear from this part of the country and

13

especially from one of the members of the Boyton-Odlum Aquatic Combination. You undoubtedly have read of the execution of the boss of the moral show, as was reported in some of the New York papers. That, however, was a false alarm, as the moral show exhibited with all its original fierceness before an immense crowd in Lima, March the 27th. Our object coming down here I presume you have heard all about. Well, as we did not succeed, and as this country fell into the hands of the Chilians, Boyton gave himself up, and is now a prisoner of war, but out on parole. He will probably have his entire freedom in a few days. He is at present on the ocean wave in the Pacific at Ancon hunting seals while I am sojourning at this place, situated in the Andes mountains, at an elevation of eight thousand feet above the level of the sea, for the purpose of benefiting my health, for when I arrived here last November I was in a precarious condition, and as I am improving I intend to remain here a year or more until I am entirely better. Boyton, however, in a short time goes to California and will resume the moral   He is also engaged by Voegeler & Co. to advertise St. Jacob's oil, and I tell you I regret I cannot continue with him. Well, since I'm up in the lofty Andes and have nothing to do, it struck me forcibly that I must write a few lines to Washington's Son of Neptune just to recall a few pleasant little instances that occurred nearly a year ago. Our exhibitions, foot of Seventh and the other in Thirteenth street, are yet fresh in my memory, as also the excursion on the Potomac, the racket in Baltimore, the midnight call when baby died, and the grand final at Atlantic City. Oh, give me back my happy days!

On one occasion I heard the captain remark that he wished that you were here (that was when we

were trying to carry out our scheme). He said
you would have been a very good addition to assist
in a new scheme he had in carrying on our intended work of destruction.

You will undoubtedly run across the captain
before the summer is out, as he has a large field
before him which no doubt will include a run on
the Potomac in the pursuits of·his new enterprise ;
so I will not say much in regard to our many
adventures.

The señoritas here are a charming lot, not handsome, but just the thing to learn Spanish from.
They do not play cards when their babies die, but
they play the guitar and flute.

I have met here several officers of the United
States Navy who know you well, and have bathed
at your establishment. They speak of you in the
highest terms, except one, who says he outrivaled
you of a nymph who was taking lessons at your
place.

The winter season is just coming in, but in this
place the thermometer hangs around sixty all the
time, and they have new potatoes every month in
the year, and new fruits coming in always.
Among them are the palta, chiramoya, grenadillas,
green figs, pomegranates, and many others too
numerous to mention. On last New Year's Day
we had pears, strawberries, fresh grapes and water-
melons. How is that for luxury ?

The peculiarities of this country are simply wonderful. The scenery, the habits and customs of
the people are truly strange to a foreigner, and
one will at once fancy himself in another world.
If you are not too busy through the summer come
down and see us once in a while and you can see
for yourself. You can easily capture a señorita
and take her back and exhibit her as a great Peru-

vian curiosity. It would be a good advertisement for your place.

I will not write any more just now, but if you answer this I shall send you an extensive letter describing our South American tour. Remember me to your clerk, whose name I've forgotten. Address "George Kiefer, Matucana." Enclose the letter and place it in another envelope and direct it to "Paymaster John Corwin, U. S. N., care U. S. Consul, Panama."

The captain sends his compliments and would like to hear from you.

Yours very sincerely,   GEORGE KIEFER.

P. S.—Boyton leaves to-day for New York via Panama, a thing to me unexpected. I presume to get out of the hands of the Chilians.

GEORGE.

These two accounts differ very materially. Boyton's own account makes himself out a fearless warrior. George Kiefer, who is a friend of Boyton and was in Peru all the time while Boyton is said to have been performing his heroic deeds, says the gallant captain was an advertising agent for St. Jacob's oil—whether to pour on the troubled waters or not is a question our readers must solve for themselves. Boyton's character as a bombastic blow-hard is sufficiently established. He has lived by his wits so long that his stay "upon the rocks" is only of short duration. Like the hawk, he keeps an eye to windward to discover some prey to pounce upon, and woe betide the man possessing either the skill to be made a tool of or the means to administer to his pleasure.

The following letters from the ex-Vice-President

to Professor Odlum may be interesting to the general reader :

P. O. address, South Bend, Ind.

ADAMS EXPRESS CO., BALTIMORE, MD.,
June 23, 1882.

MY DEAR SIR: I cannot let the occasion pass by without stating again in writing, as I have orally, how glad I was to make your acquaintance at Old Point, to receive your suggestions in the morning as to swimming, and your timely and valuable aid with my boy in the afternoon. The last *I can never forget*. And when I saw him struggling against the adverse tide, of which neither he nor I knew anything, I repented of my consent, and was immensely relieved when you made the jump and had him safely on your back. I write this note to assure you that I shall always remember you. If you think any certificate from me of the usefulness and excellence of your instructions in swimming would be of any service to you, I would very cheerfully furnish it on your informing me of your desire for it. Respectfully yours, SCHUYLER COLFAX.
Prof. R. E. ODLUM.

—

SOUTH BEND, IND., *July* 10, 1882.

MY DEAR SIR: I was very glad to find on my recent brief visit for a day to the Hygeia, at Fortress Monroe, Virginia, that you had established a swimming school at that delightful seaside resort. You have been so successful in teaching so many to swim who never swam before, and I was so impressed with your lessons to others which I witnessed, that the next time I am at Old Point I shall desire you to put me through a course, and teach me also, if I am not too old to learn. With best wishes, yours respectfully, SCHUYLER COLFAX.
Prof. R. E. ODLUM.

The dust has claimed its own, and the old man dying, left hundreds of thousands to the son, whose life the heroic Odlum saved. Professor Odlum, too, has gone to meet his reward beyond the unknown sea. The sorrow-stricken mother of the unfortunate Professor made known her intention of publishing his biography, and informed young Colfax of her intention in the following letter, naturally concluding that he would become a subscriber to the book or give a reason therefor, or a letter for publication in the same:

215 FOUR-AND-A-HALF STREET, N. W.,
WASHINGTON, D. C., *June*, 1885.
Mr. SCHUYLER COLFAX, JR., *South Bend, Indiana.*

DEAR SIR: I am the mother of Robert Emmet Odlum, who lost his life at the Brooklyn Bridge on the 19th of May last. I am in possession of a diary he kept, and by reference to it I see that he had the honor of saving your life from drowning at Fortress Monroe in the summer of 1882. You know better what he did for you than I can tell you, and as I am about to publish a biography of my unfortunate son, I write to inform you of the fact, and ask your subscription to the work. I am now sixty-four years old and in need of the money to pay my publisher. The demand for the book I am assured will be such that it will enable me to raise a fund to support me in my declining years, as well as commemorating the memory of my son, who deserved a better fate.

Please address me 215 Four-and-a-half street, northwest, and oblige, yours, truly,

CATHERINE ODLUM.

The hopeful son seems to have inherited the ingratitude as well as the fortune of his illustrious

sire. Honor and common gratitude would have
dictated a reply to the mother's letter, but no answer ever came. Perhaps he does not consider the
saving of his life a subject worth mentioning, and
doubtless the country will look upon it as an offi-
cious act on the part of Professor Odlum and will
not give him much credit therefor, especially when
his time might have been more honorably and more
profitably employed than in rescuing his life.

LETTER TO MRS. SCHUYLER COLFAX.

WASHINGTON, D. C., *July*, 1885.
Mrs. SCHUYLER COLFAX, *South Bend, Indiana.*

DEAR MADAM: Some time in June last I wrote
your son, Schuyler Colfax, informing him of the
death of my son, Robert Emmet Odlum, at the
Brooklyn bridge in May. When I remember that
my son saved the life of yours—rescuing him from
the sea in 1882 at Fortress Monroe at the peril of
his own life—I can hardly realize the motive that
causes your son to refuse to acknowledge the re-
ceipt of my letter, if nothing more. If his life
was worth saving he would be grateful to his res-
cuer, but he knows best whether the prolongation
of his existence is a subject to be thankful for,
either by himself, the community in which he lives,
or the general public. This is of course best known
to himself. I shall not argue the point with him.

My son is dead, and left me in embarrassed circumstances. His memory and the many genero
acts he performed will cause him to live in my
heart and the hearts of his friends. I have lost my
all : my property was destroyed by the Federal
army near Memphis, Tenn., my house torn down
as a military necessity, and every four-footed animal I owned in the world shot down before my eyes.

My eldest son was a member of the Eighth Missouri, one of the most famous regiments from the West in the Federal army and was killed or captured at the battle of Shiloh, for I have never heard from him since. Twenty years have rolled away, and still I have no tidings of my missing boy. His commander, Gen. Morgan L. Smith, testified that my son "was brave unto recklessness," when addressing me a letter after the war.

I have stood at the doors of Congress waiting to be repaid for my property for twelve or fourteen years. At one time a bill granting me $80,000 passed in the Senate but failed in the House; at another session it passed the House but failed in the Senate, so I have waited year after year for what was justly my own, while the amount was lying idle in the Treasury vaults. What I have suffered in the loss of my two children, and being reduced from affluence to poverty, is known only to Him who knoweth all things. I am consoled, however, by the reflection that my sons were brave and generous and did some good to others while they lived. Had your son saved the life of mine, there would have been no bounds to my gratitude, and if our financial conditions were reversed I would have come to your relief and esteemed it an honor to do so, but it takes a variety of people to make a world, and the saving of the life of your son doesn't seem to interest you much, and perhaps you know him well enough not to be too demonstrative in your feelings. As he seems to lack gratitude, which is the parent of every other virtue, you may be right in keeping silent on the subject, as you may doubtless blame, rather than thank, my son for rescuing him from a watery grave.

The son of an ex-Vice-President of the United

States, the second office in the gift of the American people, should be composed of better material, but history teaches us that great men leave no children worth speaking of. Washington left none, and your husband followed his example—so far as the public will ever be concerned in the bestowal of office. If he is the last scion of the house of Colfax, then the race is extinct.

Respectfully yours,

CATHERINE ODLUM.

How different was the conduct of Mr. T. Cooley, who appreciated the brave man who saved his life at the risk of his own. The following letter speaks for itself:

NORFOLK, VA., *July* 24, 1882.

Mr. ODLUM, *Swimming Master, Hygeia Hotel.*

DEAR SIR: I hand you herewith a little souvenir, a trifle in intrinsic value, but it represents a great deal in the more than kindly feeling that I have for you. Your timely assistance rendered me on last Thursday, it is more than likely, saved my life. I was thoroughly exhausted when my friend, Mr. Brown, called for you, and you promptly responding to his call has shown to many of the guests of the "Hygeia" the good judgment displayed by Mr. Phœbus in establishing the swimming school and employing so useful a man as yourself as its manager. I hope that it may be in my power at some time in the future, to show you in some more substantial way the grateful feelings that I have for you. In the mean time please accept the trifle with my very best wishes for your health and prosperity.

Very sincerely, T. COOLEY.

Mr. A. M. Morton, of Kentucky, who owes his

life to the gallantry of Professor Odlum, wrote him from Old Sweet Springs, W. Va., as follows :

OLD SWEET SPRINGS, W. VA.,

August 22, 1882.

Sig. R. E. ODLUM.

DEAR SIR: It affords me great pleasure to add another to the many testimonials you have received. While at Old Point I was sick and weak, and when bathing my feet were carried out by the tide, and, but for the timely assistance so promptly and gallantly rendered by you, mine might have been the fate of the unfortunate Mr. Ruff; so please accept the expressions of my profoundest gratitude, with the hope that you may live long and be blessed with health and strength to continue the good and gallant deeds which have so distinguished your past career. Again accept the thanks and good wishes of—

Yours sincerely,   A. M. MORTON.

ANOTHER GALLANT ACT.

On the 6th of August, 1882, an excursion of Knights of Pythias came from Baltimore to Fortress Monroe, and while there one of their number, G. Fred. Ruff, was drowned. The assistance rendered by Professor Odlum on that occasion will be best explained by reading the following letter :

GRAND LODGE OF MARYLAND, K. OF P.,

BALTIMORE, *August* 10, 1882,

Pythian Period XIX.

R. E. ODLUM, Esq.

MY DEAR SIR: For your services on that melancholy and never-to-be-forgotten occasion, regarding the recovery of the body of my late companion and friend, G. Fred. Ruff, I feel totally unable to pen a suitable testimonial to your distinguished abilities as a swimmer and diver, but I am satisfied, in my mind, had you reached the spot earlier you might, if life still existed, have saved him.   On the part of his associates on that unhappy trip and on behalf of the Order who loved and respected him so highly, and for the sorrowing wife and children, I return their sincere thanks for your daring and noble act, while others did all they could, but for you his remains may have not been found. You may very properly preserve such a record ; it is one that will ever endure with fadeless splendor, a pride to your family, and example of emulation to others.   Any time you are in the city you will receive a cordial welcome from me and the Order.

Very truly yours, &c.,   JAMES WHITEHOUSE,
[SEAL.]   *G. K. of R. and S.*

Professor Odlum was a man light hearted as a boy, open, free, and jovial in his disposition, and was the only living rival of Captain Webb, whose devoted friend he was, and whose untimely death he sincerely mourned.   As a teacher of swimming, he was without an equal.   His method was natural, simple, and under his instruction easily learned. Since his death the following letter has been received from ex-President Hayes, which goes to show the appreciation in which he was held as a teacher :

LETTER FROM EX-PRESIDENT HAYES.

FREMONT, OHIO, *June* 24, 1885.
DEAR MADAM: Both of our younger children attended the swimming school in Washington of your son, the late Robert Emmet Odlum.   He was

an excellent teacher, and was much esteemed by
his pupils, who heard of his death with surprise
and regret.

Sincerely,   R. B. HAYES.
Mrs. CATHERINE ODLUM,
Washington, D. C.

This is but one of many of a similar character
received by the mother of the deceased.

Many words of condolence have been received
from friends in Washington and elsewhere, sympathizing with me in this recent terrible affliction, a
few of which are herewith given: ·

FIFTH AVENUE HOTEL,
NEW YORK CITY, *May* 21, 1885.
Mrs. CATHERINE ODLUM.

DEAR MADAM: Accept my sincere sympathy in
your terrible affliction. Is there anything I can
do for you at this time? If so, command me.
Answer. Yours truly,   WARNER MILLER.

—

• CATSKILL, N. Y., *May* 20, 1885.

MY DEAR MRS. ODLUM: I have read the accounts
of your son's terrible venture, which has shocked
the civilized world to-day, and I sympathize with
you and daughter most sincerely in his death. I
know he had been a good son and brother, and that
you will feel desolate without him, and will need
more than ever the consolation of your dear church
to sustain you.

My first impulse was to go on to you for a few
days, but I scarcely knew that I could be of any
service to you. But in time of trouble I naturally
remember our long friendship, and felt that I must
at once send you few words of love and comfort
that so poorly express all I feel.

Poor Robert! with all his pleasant ways and high hopes, how sad it all is.

Give my love to Charlotte, and let me have a line to know how it is with you.

Yours faithfully,   HARRIET L. DOLSEN.

---

819 THIRD AVENUE, S. BROOKLYN,
May 29, 1885.

DEAR MRS. ODLUM: With pain I heard the sad tidings of your brave son's death, and deeply do I sympathize with you in your terrible bereavement.

Hearts that have been pierced with the sword of sorrow, pray that you may be comforted by one who never fails.

With tenderest sympathy, I remain yours truly,
KATE BENNETT.

THE ARLINGTON,
WASHINGTON, D. C., *May* 22, 1885.
Mrs. CATHERINE ODLUM.

DEAR MADAM: In the death of your son, Robert Emmet Odlum, I deeply sympathize with you, and write to offer you any aid in my power, either personal or financial. Please let me know at once how I can serve you.

Yours truly,   T. ROESSLE.

WASHINGTON, D. C., *July* 15, 1885.
Mrs. CATHERINE ODLUM.

DEAR MADAM: I understand you will shortly publish a biography of your lamented son, Prof. R. E. Odlum. Please put me down as a subscriber for one hundred copies at one dollar each. I have no doubt the work will sell readily, and the business men of Washington should patronize the work. I wish you much success in your laudable undertaking. Sincerely yours,   FRANK HUME.

OFFICE PUBLIC PRINTER,
WASHINGTON, D. C., *May* 20, 1885.
Mrs. CATHERINE ODLUM.

DEAR MADAM: Sympathizing with you in your severe bereavement, I offer my services to do anything in my power to assist you. Whatever I can do will be gladly performed.

Very truly,   S. P. ROUNDS.

—

No. 610 NINTH STREET, N. W.,
WASHINGTON, D. C., *July* 15, 1885.
Mrs. CATHERINE ODLUM.

MADAM: The death of your son was a great shock to me who knew him so well and appreciated him so highly. I did not know you, but unite with you in deploring his untimely death. The biography you will soon issue is looked for eagerly by his friends. I inclose you fifty dollars for fifty copies, at one dollar each, and I only regret I can do no more. Command me in anything I can serve you. The book will have a good sale, and I shall aid you by every means in my power in getting the work out.

I am truly your friend,
JAMES H. VERMILYA.

A PARTING WORD TO THE FRIENDS OF MY BELOVED SON.

In the hour of my supreme affliction I received offers of aid, personal and financial, from a great number of persons, whose names are engraved on my memory, and will remain while my life lasts. The list would be too long to mention them all, but I record the names of some who were his devoted friends while living and who stood by his coffin and his mother "after life's fitful fever was over." Among them I name Messrs. William

Dickson, F. K. Ward, E. D. Wright, R. M. Vanneman, Washington Nailor, J. A. Rudd, Captain E. S. Randall, of the steamer Mary Washington, Major Dye, Captain Vernon, and Charles S. Moore, whose devotion to a dead friend was most marked, who received the remains at the depot and left only when the body was laid in the vault at Mt. Olivet.

To the members of the Washington Light Infantry, for their beautiful floral tribute, I tender my sincerest thanks ; also to Messrs. Jas. H. Vermilya and Frank Hume, and to many other business men of Washington, who knowing my son personally in life remembered his aged mother after death. To each and all—friends of my unfortunate boy, named and unnamed—I tender my heartfelt thanks for each and all things they have done unto me. I cannot close without expressing my gratitude to the press of Washington for the tone of sympathy they have expressed for my son.

The demand for the first edition of this book far exceeds the supply, and a second edition will be immediately issued, in which more detailed notices will be given of many persons and incidents crowded out of this.

CATHERINE ODLUM.

.